HALLOWEEN

BITES

13 SNACK-SIZED STORIES

2024

FROM BLACK MARE BOOKS

ISBN: 978-1-959008-42-2

Blac*Mara Books,

First edition 2024

This is a work of fiction. Names, characters, places, events, locations, and incidents are either the product of the author's imagination or are used fictitiously. The author's other works may contain the use and/or mention of various products or notable institutions, some fictitious, which have been used without permission. The publication of these trademarks is not authorized, associated with, or sponsored by the trademark owners.

ISBN: 978-1-959008-422

Contents

FLANNEL
By A. B. Richards

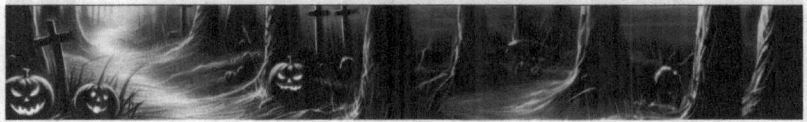

"HA! This one's perfect." I held up the red and black plaid flannel shirt to show Sue.

She rolled her eyes and sighed. "You know, Tip, when Julia set the theme for her Halloween party as 'Enchanted Forest,' she meant things like fauns and dryads. Sasquatch at the outside. I can promise you that she did *not* mean lumberjacks."

"Not so fast there. Who saved Little Red Riding Hood and her grandma from the Big Bad Wolf?"

"Nobody's gonna get that. They'll just think you're being contrarian. That your costume is scary because you're here to chop down the magical forest."

My turn for an eye roll. "You're way overthinking it."

I folded the flannel shirt over the tan pants I'd already picked out. "You got everything you need?"

"I think so. I should be able to alter this dress. Just wish they'd had a white feather boa."

"Halloween store'll probably have one. I gotta stop there and get a fake ax, anyway."

"Great. We can go to the Thai place afterwards. I'm starved."

I nodded, letting her walk ahead of me to the thrift store checkout. I sighed inwardly as I watched her hips sway with each step. She wasn't exactly my girlfriend. It was more of a 'friends with benefits' arrangement. Lately, though, I'd found myself wanting more. But I didn't want to rock the boat—if I asked for more,

I might find myself without a friend or benefits. At least we were going to the party together. That had to count for something.

The people walking by in the park had no clue I surveyed them from behind a bush. There weren't very many, because this seemed... remote. A man with a big dog jogged by. I didn't like him. The dog barked at me. Just once, as they passed.

That's what woke me up. The dream dog barking at me. I looked at my phone. Three AM. Now that I was awake, I had to pee. I peeled back the covers and sat up.

Something wasn't right. The room seemed colder than it should be. I just had the furnace inspected. Surely it wasn't broken. My skin prickled, as if hostile eyes pored over me.

"Hello? Who's there?"

I waited in tense silence, then called out to my voice assistant. "Lights!"

Every light in the house came on, and I squinted in the sudden glare. There was nobody else in my room, not even my cat, Mr. Pickles. I left all the lights on as I got up to take care of business. When I was done, I made a circuit of my home, checking that all the doors and windows were locked. They were.

Mr. Pickles was curled up on the kitchen counter, directly under the vent. Warm air gently ruffled his fur. He stretched and yawned when I came in, then tucked himself back into a ball.

Heat seemed to work everywhere but my bedroom. I'd check it out in the morning—perhaps the air filter was dirty. I grabbed an extra blanket from the linen closet and climbed back into bed. Still left the nightstand lamp on in nightlight mode, though.

By 4:30, I'd given up on going back to sleep. I got up and went to the living room and flipped on the TV. As soon as I got settled with a fluffy throw pulled up to my neck, Mr. Pickles jumped onto the couch and settled between my knees. We watched re-runs of some old black-and-white western until I fell asleep.

I shambled like a zombie through work and had a nap when I got home. After I ate dinner, I laid the flannel shirt and tan pants out on my bed. My costume from two years ago had bright red suspenders, so I got those. I'd bought a long and bushy fake beard at the Halloween store, so I put it above the shirt collar and set the ax alongside it. I had hiking boots, so I was good there.

A knit beanie. That's what I'm missing.

I thought about what Sue had said about people not getting the Little Red Riding Hood connection. *Perhaps a pelt?* I searched online for faux fur—I'd make one myself. Except that faux fur was $40/yard at the local fabric stores, and there wasn't time to get it online. *Maybe one of the $5 strips of fake fur trim? I could glue it to the ax and add some fake blood. No. Too gruesome.* Didn't want to get thrown out of the party for glorifying animal abuse.

What about... a flower? Didn't Little Red get in trouble for straying from the path to pick flowers? Poor thing. Out there all alone, lost in the deep, dark woods. Being stalked by the Big Bad Wolf. She doesn't see him, but she knows he's there. Her heart pounds with fear, her breath comes in ragged gasps as he creeps closer....

I shuddered. *Well, that was dark. Thanks, brain. I was hoping to get some sleep tonight. Why are you like this?*

I again consulted the interwebs and found multiple stores with knit beanies for sale. I drove to the closest one, and within a short time, my costume was complete.

I did a double-take when I opened my front door. I almost didn't recognize Sue in her forest nymph costume. Her skin was a pale green, and instead of hair, Spanish moss tumbled down to her shoulders from behind pointed ears. She had woven fall flowers into the cascade and attached a papier mâché bird to the shoulder of her dress. Sue had removed the pencil skirt from the silk bodice and replaced it with yards of tulle, looking like some elfin ballerina.

"Come in." I stepped aside, and she squeezed her poufy skirt through the doorway.

Sue frowned at me. "Are you okay? You look super tired."

"No." I shook my head. "Been having weird dreams and haven't been sleeping. I think I've gotten five or six hours since I saw you on Wednesday."

"You still want to go to the party? I can drive."

I held up my keys. "I'm fine. Wouldn't miss it." I picked up my ax. "Let's go."

A yowling came from the other side of the house.

"Mr. Pickles!" Sue rustled down the hall and disappeared into the guest bedroom.

There was a small courtyard between the master and guest bedrooms, and I'd put up a catio for him so he'd be safe outside watching the birds (and they'd be safe from him). *Is he stuck?*

Sue returned with a purring cat. As she got close to me, though, he hissed and leaped out of her arms.

"What's up with that? Mr. Pickles adores you." She watched him run down the hall.

"I don't think he likes the beard. You know cats don't tolerate change well."

We got in the car and headed to Rex and Mina's place.

"So, you said you've been having weird dreams? What are they about?"

If I told Sue about the blood-soaked nightmares I'd been having lately, she'd jump out of the car at the next stop sign. I shrugged. "Well. It's hard to say, exactly. I'm in the woods and it's dark and scary."

Sue's eyebrow lifted, and she playfully smacked my arm. "Like Little Red Riding Hood?"

More like the Big Bad Wolf. I am why the woods are scary. "Maybe."

I sat sideways in the chair, my legs stretched out in front of me, crossed at the ankles. Kinda hurt my back, but it just seemed... right to sit like that. I wasn't really into true crime, but I could listen to Sue talk about it. But then again, I could listen to her talk about anything.

"Guess where Jenny and I are going tomorrow?" Sue bubbled.

"Grocery store?" Rex sipped his mojito.

Sue shared a look with Mina. "Villisca! In Iowa? You know the ax murder house? We're gonna spend the night for Halloween!"

"Ewww." A woman I didn't know curled her lip. "Why would you want to do that?"

The man she was with put his arm around her shoulders. "C'mon, Sydney. Let's go over there and talk to Gloria. Did you see her latest TikTok?" He gave an apologetic smile as he turned her around, guiding her to another knot of people.

Sue leaned forward. "The murders were never solved. There's a paranormal group we're going with, and we're hoping to contact the spirits of the victims. Eight people were hacked to death in the middle of the night, and more than a hundred years later, nobody has any idea who did it."

I shrugged. "Everybody's gotta die of something."

Sue cocked her head and frowned at me. "What did you say?"

I was sober enough to recognize that I should not repeat what I said. "It's a terrible way to die for sure."

She glared at me for a long moment. I looked down and took a sip of my rum and Coke.

"Ha! It was me! I'm the Villisca Ax Murderer!" Rex grabbed my ax and stopped. "What the hell, dude? You brought an actual ax? That seems kinda messed up. Somebody might get hurt if they didn't know it was real."

"Wait, what?" Sue slapped her hands on the table. "I was with you when you bought a plastic one at the Halloween store. Why didn't you bring that one?"

"I don't know. I mean… Kinda felt dumb carrying a fake one. Yeah…" I trailed off.

"Go put it in your car," Mina growled at me. She was angry, and her heartbeat pulsed alongside the cords that stood out from her neck. Fascinated, I watched for too long.

"Now." She crossed her arms.

I shook myself. "Sorry. Of course. I didn't mean any harm."

I locked the ax in my trunk and tossed the rest of my drink in the bushes, acutely, embarrassingly aware that even the smallest amount of alcohol often short-circuited the part of my brain that filters out inappropriate remarks. I stuck with sparkling water for the rest of the night.

Sue was standoffish after my ax murder comments. I couldn't exactly blame her, but her being upset with me was almost a physical pain. I wanted to beg for forgiveness, but I knew that would only push her farther away. While she hung out with Rex and Mina, excitedly chatting about ghost hunting and murder houses, I sat by the fire with some of Rex's friends I barely knew, half-listening to them blabber about football.

While they droned on, I thought about the ax. How it would shine like a beacon in the inky forest of my dreams, lighting my way among the dark, wet trunks. The crunch of leaves and twigs under my boots. The smell of earthy, rotting leaves with hints of resinous evergreen. Notes of copper that sang through my nostrils and electrified my brain.

By 2 AM, the football crowd had either passed out or left. I patted the pocket with my car keys. "You about ready to head out, Sue?"

She hesitated. "You sure you're okay to drive? I could get an Uber. For both of us."

I raised an orange can of flavored water. "I'm fine. I only had one and a half rum & Cokes, and that was hours ago."

She didn't look too sure and seemed to be considering her options. "Alright." She turned to Rex and Mina. "Thanks for having us. I'll send you pix from Villisca."

"You'd better!"

Sue and Mina hugged each other, and Rex clapped me on the shoulder.

"Thanks. Goodnight." I waved, car keys in my hand, as we shuffled out the door.

Sue fell asleep in the car on the way home. Or maybe she just didn't want to talk to me and was pretending. Emotions jumbled inside me. Remorse. Shame. Sadness. Anger flickered at the edges.

I pulled up in the driveway and pressed the garage door opener before gently shaking her shoulder. "You coming in?"

She yawned and stretched. "I... I probably shouldn't. Early flight. I'll ping you when I get back, okay?"

"Sure. Safe travels."

It was almost a week before my phone vibrated with a text from Sue. "TIP!!!!!! OMG. You know that true crime podcast I listen to? They just did a story on the Lumberjack Killer. He hunted in Austin but LIVED with his mom HERE IN HOUSTON!!!!!! When he was convicted, she donated all his things to charity. What if you got one of his shirts?????"

"SMH. What's the diff? It's just a shirt."

"TIIIIIIP! Do you want to wear a murderer's shirt? A dead murderer?"

"Shirts don't kill people People kill people. He's dead?"

"STAHP. He was beaten to death in prison. This is serious. If you have his shirt, it's got murder residue. Maybe that's why you have bad dreams? Could be haunted BY A SERIAL KILLER!!!!"

"Murder residue? Haunted shirts? Srsly? Why would you even think this?" I fingered the hem of the flannel shirt.

Weather right now was cool but not cold, and this shirt was just the right weight. I'd been wearing it almost constantly since the party. In fact, it fit me perfectly. *This chick is starting to get on my nerves. I wish she'd just go away and quit hassling me about my clothes.* Besides, I'd gotten used to the dreams now. They weren't so bad.

Sue sent a video clip. I almost didn't watch it, but she might come to my house to badger me if I left her on read, so I clicked 'play.' A man—I assume the Lumberjack Killer—in a red and black flannel shirt was in a room not much bigger than a closet. Three chairs and a small table. A police interrogation room. He sat sideways, back against the wall, legs stretched out in front and crossed at the ankles.

A voice from an unseen man said, "Tell us about Liza Stanton."

The killer shrugged and grinned at the off-camera speaker. "Everybody's gotta die of something."

It was like Sue had physically punched me in the gut with this video. I blinked at the now still image of the leering murderer on my screen as nausea throbbed in my stomach. Clawing at my shoulder, I couldn't get that identical shirt off my body fast enough.

"Going outside to light firepit now," I typed.

Sue replied with a long string of emojis.

I picked up the shirt and some paper from the recycling bin, then went out to the deck. The firepit wasn't large, so it didn't take much wood to fill it. I crumpled the paper and tucked it around the bottom edges. As I turned to go back in to get the fireplace lighter, sun glinted on the ax that lay across the chaise lounge.

I picked it up. The handle was hard and smooth in my hand, the steel head heavy, and the blade sharp. I ran my thumb across the edge and a thin line of bright blood appeared.

Perhaps the blade was thirsty. I smeared the blood on the cold steel and smiled. This was a powerful tool.

With the ax in one hand, I could hold a life in the other, like a fragile butterfly.

I could set it free.

Or I could crush it.

And in that moment, I was God. All-powerful. Terrible. Merciful. Supreme.

I set the ax down.

Think I'll hang onto the shirt a little longer. Sue'll be here, sooner or later.

She's always been obsessed with true crime, hasn't she?

GINGERBREAD

By Artemis Greenleaf

O UR father claimed it was a family vacation, but Johan and I knew better. Dad was desperate for cash, so we loaded up the decrepit SUV and headed a couple of hours through the desert to Las Vegas.

"You guys are too old to trick-or-treat, so you should get a kick out of all the Halloween stuff going on in Vegas."

My brother and I looked at each other. We hadn't been trick-or-treating since our mom died when we were ten. This was the fall of our gap year between high school and college. It wasn't for anything fun—no backpacking across Europe or hiking the Appalachian Trail. Our dad had promised to pay for college. Then he got laid off. Now he and Brenda were struggling to keep the house.

I have no idea why he married that woman and stayed married to her. She despises us and bullies him. Anyway, Johan and I are working this year to save up money for classes and also help with the mortgage. Brenda wants to sell the house and move to an apartment. But there would be no room for us. For once, Dad stood up to her and flat out told her 'No.'

Driving into Las Vegas at night wasn't much different from driving into any other city. Until we hit the Strip. I'm glad I was not at the wheel, because all the flashing neon and blinding digital signage was overwhelming.

A giant mummy glowered from the top of the Luxor.

Flying monkeys soared around the MGM.

The balloon basket at Paris was filled with ghosts.

An angry Minotaur paced in front of Caesar's Palace.

The pirate ship at Treasure Island had a literal skeleton crew.

The Sphere was a jack-o'-lantern.

It was too much!

We were staying some place off the Strip. Way off. It was walkable, but it was a long walk.

We sat in the car with Brenda while Dad checked us into some generic budget motel. When we walked into the room, I immediately wished I'd brought my own sheets. The multicolored patterned carpet had a big stain that I really hoped was coffee and not blood. One of the beds tilted at a slight angle, and the other had a deep well in the middle that not even the 60s flower print bedspread could disguise.

I knew there was no budget for two rooms, and anyway, I didn't want to get stuck in a 'girls' room' with Brenda. At our age, it might be weird being in the same bed with my brother, but at least I could trust him not to smother me with a pillow while I was sleeping.

"Who's hungry?" Dad beamed at us.

Brenda licked her lips. "Which buffet are we going to?"

His face fell. "Actually... I was thinking we'd just walk to the little café across the street."

Brenda scowled.

"M-maybe tomorrow? I'm really tired."

"Sure, Dad," my brother said. "Be good to stretch my legs."

I was starving and wanted to eat now. And of course, if it thwarted Brenda, I was all in. "Me, too."

We all turned to Brenda, knowing if she pitched a fit, Dad would cave.

She looked like she'd been sucking lemons. "Fine. For tonight."

Great. Tomorrow, she's going to badger Dad into eating at one of the expensive buffets he can't really afford.

We headed downstairs and jaywalked to the Black Forest Café. When Dad opened the door, an animatronic werewolf growled at us as his eyes glowed red. Brenda jumped. Johan and I snickered.

The waitress reminded me of our grandma. She was pleasantly plump, with square glasses. After seating us at a booth against a window, she handed out laminated menus and wrote down our drink order.

As she walked away, I took in the ambiance. Looked like it had been there for decades longer than I'd been alive. Someone had painted murals of castles, forests, and armored knights. At least I think that's what they were. I pulled out my phone and surreptitiously snapped a few pix.

"Greta! What are you doing?" Brenda slapped her menu on the table.

"You know she takes pictures of everything, right, Brenda?" Johan continued studying his own menu.

"Like that's some kind of excuse!" She glared at the back of Dad's menu while he studiously ignored her.

She waited several seconds for him to reply before she gave up. "Don't you dare post that on your social media accounts until we get home. No need to advertise we're out of town."

I rarely posted my pictures on the socials. I took them to help me remember activities, as ideas for stories, or references for drawing.

I flashed her a fake smile and nodded.

When we got back from dinner, I laid towels down on top of the bed and slept on them in my clothes. It felt like I'd only just fallen asleep when a jag of light from the opening door woke me. I saw Dad leave through blurry eyes. Guess he was trying to get his casino streak started early.

When I woke up around eight, Johan was already dressed and reading a book. Brenda had gone off somewhere. *Good riddance.*

I put on fresh clothes, brushed my teeth, and we went out for the day. The Black Forest Café was open 24 hours, so we stopped there to eat. This motel didn't offer a breakfast, and I'm not sure I would have trusted the food if it did. We searched our phones for activities while we waited for our meals to arrive.

"What about this?" I held up my phone.

"Gingerbread's?" He cocked his head, skepticism in his voice.

"I know it looks like it's for little kids with all that fake candy stuck on it, but the reviews say it's one of the best under-21s in town. And they have a huge Halloween party tonight."

Johan sighed. "Well, I guess we can look for costumes while we're out. If nothing else, there's gotta be a Target or something around."

"Gotta be."

I messaged Dad. "Having breakfast at Black Forest. How's it going?"

The food arrived before he replied. I didn't see his message until we paid the bill. "At the Nugget. Up $200!!!"

Maybe he can afford Brenda's buffet blitz after all. "Good luck!"

We bought day passes for the monorail at the Sahara Station and set out to explore. The clouds over the desert looked like an oil painting, so I snapped a few pictures of those. The train runs on the back side of the casinos, so we didn't see too many decorations, but I got some sick shots from where it winds between the golf course and the Sphere.

Dad messaged both of us around six. "Meet at Ceasar's Palace for dinner buffet?"

I initially was eager to go. Johan looked it up on his phone and showed me.

No way I was dropping a Benjamin on a meal, and I wouldn't let Dad pay for it, either. He came here to make some extra money, not flush it down the toilet. Literally. *Eww.*

Johan agreed.

"Sorry Dad. Already ate. Going to check out some Halloween parties. Don't wait up."

Of course, we'd seen some incredibly scary costumes in shops on the Strip, but they cost about the same as the tuition for my first semester of school. We found a Halloween store on a slightly less beaten track—merch was picked over, since it was the day of—but everything that was left was on sale.

I bought a long green wig, a witch hat, and some black and orange striped knee socks. Johan got a neck gaiter thing that you pull up over your nose that made him look like a zombie. He found some zombie glasses to go with it—the image printed facing out on the lenses was pretty gruesome, but Johan said he couldn't really see it from the inside—they just gave everything a yellowish tint. Hopefully, these get-ups would be good enough, as Gingerbread's required a costume for entry.

Admission was half price between seven and nine. We were sure there'd be a line, so we started working our way over to the club. We'd seen the pictures, but I was not prepared for what was waiting for us when we got there.

A machine belched clouds of thick mist. Eerie green lights flickered and swirled in the fog. People who I figured must be Cirque de Soleil understudies were dressed in one-piece body-suits that covered them from head to toe. Some climbed on giant cobwebs and did acrobatic tricks. Others bent themselves into disturbing, boneless shapes.

Gingerbread's was three stories tall. Lights underneath the huge plastic candies on the roof alternated between flashing in patterns and random pops of light. The texture on the building really looked like crisp gingerbread decorated with white icing. Yellow, green, and blue swirled candy canes formed the window frames, and the shutters were made of pink wafer cookie sticks. Colored lights from the upper windows throbbed to the beat of a dance track almost contained by the outer walls.

The number of people there to get into the club was much more than we expected, but the place was so huge I wasn't worried about getting in. A few street magicians worked the crowd. A pair of showgirls led a small tiger on a golden leash and posed for selfies. Entertained by the performers, we waited for forty-five minutes until the doors opened.

Once the line started moving, it kept moving, as the electric gingerbread house swallowed the partygoers. I noticed the bouncer was giving people different hand stamps after studying their IDs, but I couldn't figure out a pattern. Maybe it was just like trading cards or something. I assumed some meant 'under 21' but I wasn't sure.

The place was a maze of small and large venues with various styles of music in each. Normally, I enjoy Halloween, but the costumed crowd moving around in the dimly lit rooms gave me a horror movie vibe. I seriously doubted the werewolf that just passed by was an actual werewolf, but the guy in the killer clown outfit seemed like he really could be a killer. I wished we'd come on a normal day.

There was a finger food buffet on the second floor, so we got our dinner there and sat at a small table in the bar area to eat. I held our spot while Johan fetched us some sodas. He was almost back when a pretty brunette about our age wearing a Playboy Bunny outfit bumped into him, making him spill the drinks.

"Oh my god! I am *so* sorry! I can't believe I'm such a klutz. Let me replace those. It's the least I can do. What were you having?"

Johan told her, and she trotted to the bar. A man in a black polo with 'Gingerbread's' embroidered on it seemed to materialize out of nowhere to clean the mess.

I had given up hope on the girl returning when she finally showed up with fresh sodas. "Sorry about the wait. The bar was slammed. I'm Linda, by the way."

Johan stared at her a little too long. I kicked him under the table. "I'm Greta, and this is my brother, Johan. Are you from around here?"

Linda nodded. "Grew up here. How about you guys?"

We, well, mostly Johan, chatted with her while we ate. He took his phone out to show her something, then set it down.

I don't like to drink while I'm eating—I'm weird that way—but Johan was down to the ice cubes by the time his plate was empty.

He got up to bus his dirty dishes, then grabbed the edge of the table.

"What's wrong?" I put my hand over his.

Johan shook his head. "Nothing. Just stood up too fast."

Then he swayed on his feet.

"You need to sit down." I guided him to his stool.

Johan clutched his middle and groaned. "Think I'm gonna puke."

"I'll get help." Linda paused between us, a hand on each of our shoulders. "Be right back."

Two men in Gingerbread's uniform shirts came and helped Johan up. One on each side, they walked him to a hidden elevator. We all went down into a basement, and the doors opened to over-bright fluorescent lights. I squinted and followed them.

Crap. Johan's phone is still on the table.

Thinking Linda was behind me, I turned to ask her if she would mind going back upstairs and grabbing the device, but she was nowhere to be seen. I guess it wasn't really strange she didn't come down to the medical area with us. It's not like we were friends or anything. Whatever. I couldn't deal with her or the stupid phone right now.

We came to a door marked 'EMS' and went inside.

The place wasn't all that different from the ER of the small hospital at home—a front desk, a few chairs, a TV on a news channel, and some curtained off areas I assumed were beds. The men took Johan toward the bays.

"Ma'am?" the woman behind the desk called out. I looked around the room, but I was the only other person in sight.

"Me?"

She smiled. "Yes. I need you to fill out some forms." She held out a clipboard.

"Uh… sure, I guess. Listen, could you call our dad while I'm doing this?"

"Of course."

I reached down near her phone for a pad of sticky notes and wrote the number. She started pressing buttons as I sat down with the paperwork.

At first, the questions seemed pretty normal. Name, contact info, allergies. Then they got weird.

"Excuse me, but my brother doesn't wear a bra. I think you gave me the wrong paperwork."

"No, those are for you."

"But you're not treating me, and even if you were, why would you need to know my cup size?"

The door opened and a man in an expensive suit strutted in, followed by two grim-faced men who towered over him. The air seemed to get stuck in my throat, and my brain was shouting, 'Run! Run! Runrunrunrunrunrun!' From Suit's black eyes to imported Italian shoes, evil radiated off him, kinda like stink lines from a cartoon.

Both of the apparent bodyguards had full sleeve tattoos, variations on a skeleton in long robes, wearing a crown. One had praying hands, the other carried a scythe and a globe.

I wasn't going anywhere without Johan, and these guys had nothing to do with us. I shrank against my seat and focused on the papers.

I could feel Suit's eyes sliding over me, leaving slimy trails like malevolent slugs. After a moment, he sauntered up to the front desk. "*Hola*, Bella. You have my merchandise?"

"Yes, sir. Just go straight back."

Suit and his entourage stepped into the treatment area. I pretended to study the forms while I strained to hear what was being said.

Suit: "Ha! *Perfecto!*"

Someone mumbled.

Johan: "What are you doing with that? No!"

I got to my feet, but one of the bodyguards appeared in the aisleway to block me.

"What are they doing to my brother?" I shouted at him.

From behind the curtains, Johan called out, "Greta? Help me!"

"Leave him alone!" I yelled, uselessly. I turned my body so that it blocked Evil-dee's view as I slid my phone out of my pocket to dial 9-1-1. *Dammit. No signal. Too much concrete down here. Now what?*

A clatter behind me made me whip around so fast I almost dropped my device. Evil-dum was pushing Johan, who was strapped to a gurney. Suit had a big syringe full of blood, and I noticed a bandage on my brother's arm. *Why are they wearing headlamps?*

"Where are you taking him?" I shouted and tried blocking the doorway. Evil-dee just laughed, then grabbed my hair and jerked me around, propelling me along in front of him.

"Don't worry, *chula*, you're going too." Suit chuckled somewhere behind me.

We turned a corner, and about ten feet away was a metal door with a wheel on it, as if from a ship. Suit moved forward and began turning the wheel. "Did you know there's 600 miles of tunnels below Vegas? Thousands of... people live there. Like a whole underground city."

Fear skittered across my skin with icy feet.

Suit stopped turning and pulled the door open. A scant amount of light from the corridor bled into the inky blackness. An odor drifted out of the dark. Dampness and rot. Death and decomposition. There was something bad in those tunnels, and nothing good was going to come of us setting foot in there.

Evil-dee pushed me through the doorway. I tripped over the high threshold, but his painful grip on my hair kept me from falling. He then used his free hand to lift one end of Johan's gurney. I thought that while his attention was divided, I might have a window of opportunity.

I reached up and grabbed his pinky finger, jerking it outward and up. Instead of him letting go, he slammed me into the tunnel wall hard enough to knock the wind out of me. It was small consolation, as I gasped and wheezed, that I had been able to turn my head so my nose didn't get broken. I could feel the bruise swelling on my cheekbone, though.

Suit let out a stream of what were probably curse words, but they streamed by faster than my limited Spanish could comprehend them.

"Don't damage the merchandise!"

The three men's headlamps clicked on once the stretcher had cleared the doorway. Suit pulled the door shut and spun the wheel on this side. The tunnel was nothing special. I'd seen the eight-foot-tall concrete box sections plenty of times in road work sites. It seemed to slope slightly downward, and after a short time, we came to a T-intersection. Evil-dum pushed the gurney to the right.

Somewhere up ahead, water dripped into a pool and the sound magnified and echoed off the cement. The reek of something dead got stronger, making my stomach churn. The feeling of existential dread deepened to the point I could not have taken another step into the foreboding dark of my own free will. Evil-dee relentlessly shoved me along.

I glanced at Johan from time to time. He was completely limp, his head lolling with each bump or turn. My mind raced from one bad possibility to the next. Suit had referred to me as 'merchandise.' And he had said the same thing about Johan when he greeted the receptionist. Did this tunnel end up at the airport, where he'd jet us away to some sordid future? Sell us as slaves in some distant country? Force us to be drug mules? Prostitutes?

I couldn't think about those grim possibilities now. If I was focusing on that, I would miss any chances of escape.

We took another branch of the tunnel. This one looked newer than the one we'd just left, and the upward slope was steep enough that my breath came faster and sweat beaded on my forehead. After perhaps thirty yards, the floor leveled off. The stench of rotting meat was almost unbearable now. Something in the dark beyond the headlamps made a deep, slobbery growl.

Suit raised his hand. "This is good."

The henchmen stopped. Evil-dum unbuckled Johan. Wet footsteps splatted toward us. Evil-dum cranked up one end of the stretcher, so Johan was sitting up. He shook his head and mumbled.

My fight-or-flight response had kicked in before we even entered the tunnels, and my hands trembled from the adrenaline.

Slap. Slap. Slap.

The footfalls got closer, and my heart rate got faster.

Slap. Slap. Slap.

Whatever was coming stopped at the edge of the light. I felt like I was going to jump out of my skin.

"See what I've brought you?" Suit gestured toward my brother. "I think you'll really like this one. Our standard agreement applies, of course."

"Of course," the thing rasped. And stepped into the glare of the headlamps.

I lurched backward against Evil-dee, and most of my hair slipped out of his hand. He seemed too focused on the horror before us to notice.

The narrow beams fell on something more or less human-shaped. Its arms were too long and head too big. The creature was almost as tall as the tunnel.

Worst of all, it had no skin. Red-tinged ooze coated its body and dripped onto the floor. Unlidded yellow eyes flicked from Suit to Johan, and a sharp-toothed grin spread over its raw face.

I couldn't decide what to do—scream? run?—so I stood there like a quivering lump, trying not to throw up.

My brother groaned softly, and the creature took a step closer, reaching out a slimy claw.

If I didn't do something now, it would be too late. I sucked in as much of the dank air as I could, then ran at Suit, shoving him into the arms of the monster. Time slowed down and my feet seemed to be stuck in tar. Evil-dee and Evil-dum rushed toward Suit. I shoved Johan's stretcher, and it rolled down the tunnel, picking up speed on the way.

Screams and the squelching sounds of tearing flesh bounced off the concrete behind us as I fled into the dark after Johan.

The gurney had crashed into the wall at the bottom of the rise. I helped my brother up, and he leaned on me as we stumbled through the tunnels. I used my phone to light our way, but the blackness was so intense it barely cut through.

After what felt like hours of wandering almost blind, we came across a man sitting on the floor, propped up against the wall. A syringe with a needle and a foot-long strip of cloth lay next to him. He lifted his head and regarded us with half-closed eyes.

"Up." He pointed to the ceiling.

Johan was finally getting his legs back and had stopped leaning on me. "Sure, dude. Thanks."

We hurried past. There was a faint sound of people talking. It got louder, quickly, as we moved down the tunnel. It wasn't long before we came to a ladder—metal bars embedded into the cement. The talking was coming from above there.

"Up?" Johan asked.

"May as well. Gotta get out of here somehow."

We climbed the ladder, and it took both of us pushing on the manhole cover to raise it up and out of the way. We squinted in what seemed like an unbearable brightness as we found ourselves behind some bushes in a large park. Johan pushed the metal plate back into place.

A golf ball whizzed past my ear.

"Hey! Get off the course, you dumb kids!"

"Sorry!" I shouted to the group of four men in plaid pants as we hurried to a paved path.

We got turned around a few times, but finally found our way to the street.

"Where are we?" Johan scanned the environs.

"Doesn't matter. I'll just open Maps and… crap. I'm out of data. No internet."

"Well, at least *you* have your phone."

I searched the area, hoping to find something familiar. "Wait! Isn't that the 'Welcome to Fabulous Las Vegas' sign over there?"

"Yeah, it is."

"Okay. We were here earlier. Let me open my camera roll, and we'll see what's next." I found the photo of the sign. The following image was of an elderly biker on a trike in front of the Harley Davidson store.

I looked right. "That looks like the airport."

Johan and I started walking left.

We passed the motorcycle shop. Then the Pinball Hall of Fame, where I'd snapped a pic of a man juggling on stilts.

"Wait!" Johan pointed. "Manalay Bay. The Luxor's just on the other side."

"We can get the monorail and head back to the motel!"

"You think Dad'll believe us?"

"I don't know, but I'm sure he'll know what to do."

We half-jogged to the station and bought our tickets. My phone buzzed as we were getting on the train.

"Dad!" It was still early in the morning and there was only one other person in the car.

"Where have you been? You said you'd be out late, but I've been so worried!"

I told him how Johan had been roofied at Gingerbread's, and that we'd managed to escape. I didn't mention Suit or the skinless monster.

"What? I'm calling the cops. Brenda and I will meet you at the Sahara Station, then we're going straight to the police. They've gotta put a stop to that, and I mean now! How many other kids didn't get away?"

I thought about the stench in the tunnel. Probably a lot.

When we got off the train, Dad and Brenda were there. Both of us ran to Dad and threw our arms around his neck, one on either side of him. He hugged us so hard I could barely breathe.

When he finally let go, he said, "The police are waiting downstairs. You tell them what you told me." He brushed his fingers across my hair near the nasty bruise on my cheek. "If I ever get my hands on the monster that did this to you…"

Four LVPD officers waited in the drop off area of the Sahara. Johan and I began telling our story.

Screeching tires caused all of us to look up in unison. A white Mercedes had hooked a U-turn in the middle of the road and was now barreling down on us.

I locked eyes with the driver. It was Suit. But it wasn't. Couldn't have been. Suit was dead, wasn't he? And yet… His proportions seemed off. But what made me want to scream was his eyes… his yellow, staring eyes.

Someone grabbed my shoulder and yanked me out of the way. There was a horrible wet crunch, then a heavy thud.

As I sat up on the pavement, I looked from Dad to Johan to the four cops.

Brenda hadn't made it out of the way.

"Popcorn?" Dad set a glass mixing bowl of the stuff on the coffee table.

He hit play on the remote, and the movie started.

Dad loved movies. I was glad he had this fancy wide-screen TV to watch them on now. Although he wouldn't have much time anymore. He'd gotten a new job and had to travel a lot.

When school began next week, Johan and I would be commuting to save on housing expenses.

Don't get me wrong. I would never have wished a grisly death on Brenda. True, I wanted her gone. But not that way.

However, with her sacrifice, the life insurance payment was more than enough for dad to wipe out the mortgage and spruce the place up a little.

It took a while, but he's happier than I've seen him in a very long time.

Police had broken up the human trafficking ring at Gingerbread's, but they never caught Suit. But neither Johan nor I wanted relive that experience, so we kept our mouths shut.

Life seemed good right now. Really good.

If I only could get the nightmares to stop.

Keys to the Castle

By A. B. Richards

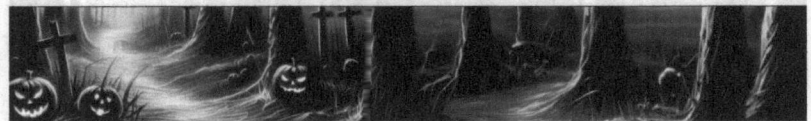

REDWOODS loomed off the sides of the road, casting deep shadows over the bracken that clumped between them. I shivered, half expecting to see gnomes sitting on the rocky out-croppings, or fairies flitting among the ferns as I drove through the tunnel of otherworldly conifers.

I suppose the Victorians started it. They wanted to paint naked ladies, but that was too scandalous, so they painted tiny naked women with wings and called them fairies. Pretend naked women were A-okay, actual naked women, no way. Then came the cutesy cartoons.

Fae are dangerous. People forget that.

It wasn't long before the giant trees were behind me, and the road began to wind its way up the mountain. I clucked to my decade-old Corolla as it struggled up the incline. *Hope I don't have to get out and push.* When my 30-year marriage exploded into a messy divorce, I fled the city and moved in with my mom in rural Northern California—she was starting to need a little help, anyway. After 25 years as a homemaker, I was now back in the labor market.

Should I pull over and read the directions again? Cell service was too unreliable in the mountains to use a navigator app, so I'd printed out the steps.

Wait! There's a sign. Chateau de Colombe 3 Miles with an arrow pointing left. I made the turn and the fluttering in my stomach increased to a fever pitch—I was nervous as a long-tailed cat in a room full of rocking chairs. It had been decades since I had done a job interview. *Would they like me? Would I come off as an id-*

iot? Should I just go back to town and take my chances with the thrift shop clerk position?

Having made better time than expected, I was now half an hour early. The driveway to Dove's Travel Plaza, a gas station-restaurant combo, yawned to my right. I pulled in. *Perhaps I could wait here and grab a cup of coffee? No, I already have the jitters.* At any rate, I needed to avail myself of the facilities.

I came out of the restroom and wandered into the mostly empty diner. A woman about my age finished taking an order from one of two occupied tables and nodded to me on her way to the back. "Seat yourself, hon."

I climbed onto a stool at the counter. The server reappeared from the kitchen and handed me a menu. I scanned the appetizers and frowned at the a la cartes. Everything was either too greasy or too sweet, and I didn't want to toss my cookies at the interviewer. The waitress hovered nearby, so as soon as I closed the laminated listing, she was in front of me.

"I'll just have an iced tea."

"You alright, hon?" She picked up the menu.

"Yeah, yeah. I'm a little early for an interview."

"At the castle? I'm sure you'll get it." Her black plastic nametag read 'DIANE' in white letters.

"Oh? Why's that?" *She doesn't know the first thing about me.*

"They're always hiring over there. Lotta churn."

"Why is that?"

Diane shrugged as she picked up a pitcher and poured tea and ice into an oversized red tumbler. "Don't really know. They get the job, work there a month or two, then the castle's hiring again." She leaned in, then looked over her shoulder. In a hushed tone, she said, "I heard the place is haunted."

Haunted, is it? Wouldn't be the first time I'd put up with ghosts. "Well, old places can be spooky."

She nodded and set the glass on a paper coaster before scurrying away to check on the other table. I drank about half the tea, paid my bill, and got back on the highway.

The driveway wasn't impressive, but the black sign with elaborate gold scrollwork insisted the resort lay to my right. I swallowed hard as I turned down the lane. The rugged scenery was spectacular, but I nearly ran off the road when I drove around a blind curve and Chateau de Colombe—Dove Castle—came into view.

I'd researched the place before applying. It had been deconstructed at its original site in the Loire Valley in France and rebuilt here, ghosts and all, apparently. The internet teemed with pictures of the resort. But to see it in person… it took my breath away. White limestone towers gleamed above manicured formal gardens. October frosts had bitten the lawn and many of the plants had shed their leaves for the winter, but the stand of lodgepole pines nearby was a deep green.

This place was the cat's pajamas! I pulled onto the shoulder and snapped a few pix. After all, I may never make it up here again.

I continued to the parking lot and went inside the castle. The receptionist, a young woman with her dark hair swept into a severe chignon, smiled at me. "Checking in?"

"No. I'm Corrie Greer. I have an interview at 2:00."

"Ah, yes. Mr. Beardsly's expecting you." She handed me a clipboard. "If you could just fill out these forms, front and back?"

Hadn't I already filled out a jillion forms online? "Of course." I took the papers and sat in one of the overstuffed leather armchairs.

The first two pages were pretty standard, but the third was a non-disclosure agreement. *What the heck happens at Dove Castle Resort that requires an NDA?* I tapped the end of my pen on my thigh. *Do they have some crazy proprietary products? Of course: Celebrities. Bet they get a lot of celebs up here who want their privacy. That makes sense.* I signed the NDA and returned the clipboard to the receptionist.

I read and re-read the copies of my resume while I waited. The crucial question I was sure he'd have was about the two-and-a-half-decade gap in my employment. I wouldn't mention the divorce. The wounds were still too raw. I'd simply say that once the kids left the nest, I wanted something to occupy my time. That was at least partially true.

The Rococo gilt-edged clock that perched imperiously on the mantelpiece taunted me with each tick of its minute hand. Twenty of those ticks had passed since I handed in my forms, and I was getting antsy.

I nearly jumped out of the chair when a door off to the left of the receptionist's desk opened and a seeming lumberjack stepped through. He was probably 6'4" and his tailored suit accentuated his broad shoulders and narrow hips. The man-bun topping his head was more primal warrior than hipster, as was his neat, blue-black beard. I guessed he was in his early forties.

"Corrie?"

"Yes." I got to my feet. "That's me."

"Come on back to my office." He held out his hand. "I'm Indigo. Indigo Beardsly. It's a pleasure to meet you."

I gave him a firm shake. "Likewise."

His work area was spacious, and the furniture more modern than that in the lobby. I took a seat in an upholstered chair, clutching my resume.

"So, Corrie. Why do you want to join our team?"

"My kids are grown and I'm ready for a new challenge. I did take some time off, but I have a strong background in hospitality."

Indigo stroked his beard as his eyes scanned the copy of my resume on his desk. "Yes. Yes, you do. And you moved here from Houston?"

"Yes. To be closer to my mother."

A broad grin revealed Indigo's ultra-white teeth. "Family is important to us here at Dove Castle."

"I'm pleased to hear that."

"The salary is $80k, firm. Plus all the usual bennies—medical, dental, 401K, paid vacay."

80. Thousand. Dollars? Shut your mouth and act like that's normal. "Okay." I nodded slowly, as if deciding whether the offer was acceptable.

"Great! When can you start?"

"Well, I, uh, have a few things to finish up from the move. Next week?"

"Fantastic! See you Monday. Trina at the front desk will give you the onboarding paperwork. Just fill it out and bring it with you then." He got to his feet.

I followed his lead, and he shook my hand again. Before I knew it, I was in my car with a folder full of forms. How had I gotten hired for an $80,000 job in a five-minute interview?

As I drove down the winding mountain road, I thought about what Diane had told me—lots of churn. Is that why the meeting finished so fast? He wasn't expecting me to be working here long and only wanted to get it over with? Could be that's his usual style, and it explains the high turnover rate—he doesn't take the time to hire the right personnel.

I had only been at the Dove for two weeks when Indigo called me into his office.

"Corrie, you've been doing a great job."

Is there a but *coming?* "Thank you."

"I'm going to have to go to the headquarters in France. Be gone for a month, and I need you to take the reins while I'm away."

Am I ready for this? What if I screw something up? Then who will hire me? "Of course."

He swiveled in his chair, gesturing to a shelf full of 3-ring binders. "I'll be mostly offline. If you have any questions that Trina can't answer, consult the manuals."

My mouth had gone dry. I tried to swallow and made an embarrassing gulp-squelch. *Great.* "I'll do that."

Indigo rose and pulled a heavy set of keys from his pocket, picked through them, and held a small brass one out toward me. "These are the keys to everything in the castle. There is a storage room in the basement." He waggled the key. "Don't go in there. Had some earthquake damage a few years ago, and it was never fully repaired. Building's not gonna collapse or anything, but there's a lotta junk lying around. Not safe to enter without steel-toed boots. Who knows? Might even be snakes."

"Got it. Stay out of the old basement storage room."

He draped his sport coat over his arm and pulled out the handle of a wheeled suitcase I hadn't noticed when I came in. "Alright. Off to the airport. See you in a month."

Indigo wasn't one to beat around the bush. "Sure. Safe travels."

Once he was out of sight, I took a deep breath. *He's probably going now because it's off season. Not much to do. You've got this. You always land on your feet.*

The summer crowd was long gone, and it was too early for folks wanting to nip out of town during Thanksgiving or Christmas holidays.

I sat on the leather sofa near the receptionist's desk. "So, Trina? When does it usually pick up around here? It's been awfully slow since I started."

She gave me a prim smile. "Halloween's not exactly a time people want to drive up twisty mountain roads in the dark to a resort." She shrugged. "Maybe if we offered pumpkin facials or hosted parties with laboratory elixirs bubbling in beakers."

But they might come for a castle ghost tour. Not that it necessarily mattered, but we were fresh out of spirits. If there were any ghosts haunting the place, they hadn't made an appearance since I'd come on board. *Perhaps they knew they wouldn't scare me.*

Still begged the question of why so many assistant managers before me had up and quit. So far, it seemed like a cushy job. I got up to wander around the grounds again, on the off chance something needed managing.

So often as I went through my day, that small brass key shone up at me, seemingly more polished than any of the others. It drew my thoughts to the forbidden room. *Surely there was nothing interesting in there—just junk. But why did he tell me about it?*

I strolled into the front lobby and leaned on Trina's desk. "What do you think about closing up early? We've had three guests all week, and no one is scheduled for today or tomorrow. "

Her eyes widened. "No. Mr. Beardsly wouldn't like it."

How would he find out? "Okay. Only a suggestion. Didn't know if you had little kids to take trick-or-treating tonight."

She gave me such an odd look that I was sorry I asked. "Listen, Ms. Greer. Not trying to be rude. But I can't lose my job. I just do what I'm told and don't rock the boat."

"I understand. But if you want to leave early, I'll claim responsibility."

"Perhaps if I was on salary and not hourly...."

I decided to check on the spa manager. The views from the terrace where the massage tables were set up were spectacular. Near the elevator, I dropped that ridiculous ring of keys. The shiny brass one somehow separated itself from the others. I took it as a sign and pressed the down arrow instead of the up. I'd only been down there once, when I got the Day 1 Grand Tour.

The basement had been gouged into the bones of the mountain. Some walls were finished with wood and steel. Others were raw stone. It contained the expected things—HVAC, elevator equipment, and laundry room, etcetera.

My footsteps echoed off the hard surfaces as I moved into the bowels of the resort. "Hello?"

No reply, just the humming of machines.

I took a few more steps. *Is that really an echo, or is someone following me?*

As soon as I changed my walking pattern, the 'echo' got ahead of me. "Hello? Who's down here?"

No answer.

I searched the entire area, checking under or behind every piece of machinery. As far as I could tell, I was alone. *But those footsteps—had I imagined them?*

Finding myself in the dim and distant end of the basement, I looked around. *Wait. There's a door.* I tried turning the knob, but it wouldn't budge. No doubt in my mind this was the lock that belonged to the shiny brass key.

Should I open it? Indigo is thousands of miles away in France. He'd never know… I searched the darkened corner for cameras and found none.

If there is only junk in there what would be the harm of opening the door? I wouldn't have to go inside, just take a peek through the doorway. Curiosity killed the cat, but satisfaction brought it back.

A clang sounded from the laundry room. I ran to it and flung open the door, sure I'd catch whoever had been following me.

It was empty.

Nothing out of place.

Must have been the water pipes. No telling how old they are. I took advantage of the bright light, locating the brass key on the heavy ring. With a deep breath, I crept back to the gloomy corner.

The door clicked open as soon as the key slipped into the lock. I couldn't see anything in the dark room. But the foul odor that rolled out made me gag.

Spoiled meat.

Excrement.

Metal.

I grabbed my phone and lit up the area with my flashlight.

The shock of what I saw was a baseball bat to the abdomen.

I recognized the faces on a couple of the fresher corpses from the 'Employee of the Month' plaque. The other assistant managers hadn't quit or been fired. Looked like they were all here. Or at least parts of them were, in various stages of decomposition. Some hung from hooks suspended from the ceiling. Others were scattered in pieces on the floor.

A violent shock to my back sent me tumbling into the abattoir. I wretched as my hands made contact with the crusty dried blood that coated the entire room.

I scrambled to my feet as Indigo Beardsly slammed the door shut behind us.

He stroked that blue-black beard and chuckled. "I did tell you not to come in here. Little reverse psychology, though. Works every time."

"You? You killed all the assistant managers?"

"Everybody's gotta have a hobby." He laughed again.

I raised an eyebrow. "You need to open that door and let me go right now."

"Oh, Corrie. You know I can't do that."

"Yes, you can."

"No."

I sighed. "Don't say I didn't warn you."

My fingernails narrowed and hardened into scythe-sharp claws and my human skin turned to black cat fur even as he charged me. I buried my fangs in his throat and locked my jaw until he stopped struggling.

Trina brought a cup of coffee, cream, no sugar, into my new office.

"Thanks. How many reservations do we have this week?"

"Twenty-three."

"Excellent. Are you doing okay? You look a little peaked."

The receptionist shuddered. "The police have no idea where Indigo—Mr. Beardsly—is. What if he returns?"

I leaned back in my chair. "No chance. I know it's a lot to digest, but he's gone for good. Not to be saucy, but I'm sure he can't stomach the sight of the Dove any longer. The cops won't find hide nor hair of him."

She narrowed her eyes. If she suspected I knew what happened to Indigo, she was keeping it to herself.

I rubbed my belly. Hadn't eaten in a week now, I was so stuffed. Indigo had been a big man. Tough and stringy, too. Maybe I'd be up for a light dinner tonight.

Fae are dangerous. People forget that.

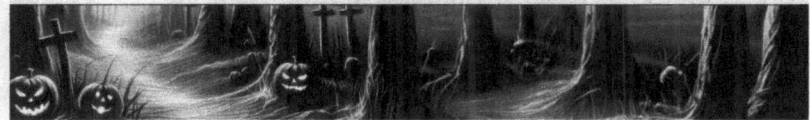

FAIREST
By Holly Dey

RUBY Lawson faced the judge, making steady eye contact as she spoke. "Your honor, at this preliminary hearing, the prosecution wants you to believe that Findlay Regis is a vicious, cold-blooded killer. A danger to society. But that is the farthest thing possible from the truth. Findlay acted in self-defense. He is nothing but a loving husband who has only the safety and well-being of his wife at heart. Vivien Lumi was by no means an innocent victim. She stalked her stepdaughter and attempted to murder her on four separate occasions. The defense will prove, well beyond a shadow of a doubt, that Findlay Regis is not a monster, but a hero." She paused to look around the courtroom. "I'd like to call my first witness, Dr. Wilhelm Jacobs."

A man with a pinched, aquiline nose and bushy grey hair got up to be sworn in. Ruby spent as much time establishing his credentials as she could without putting the judge to sleep. "Now, Dr. Jacobs. I am aware that Mrs. Lumi was never your patient, so it isn't possible for you to accurately diagnose her. However, as an expert in Cluster B personality disorders, you are certainly capable of determining whether or not her behavior is consistent with having a malignant narcissistic personality disorder. Is that accurate?"

"It is."

"You have reviewed her file. Would you please explain what a malignant narcissistic personality disorder is?"

"A person with narcissistic personality disorder tends to have an exaggerated sense of self-importance, and craves admiration, and will engage in deception to receive it, if necessary. They also have little or no empathy for others. If you add paranoia and the other dark tetrad traits—Machiavellianism, sadism, psychopathy—you get a malignant narcissist. According to her file, Ms. Lumi reportedly suffered from visual and auditory hallucinations—she believed her mirror spoke to her."

"Would you define 'Machiavellianism,' please?"

"It is where someone is manipulative and amoral, with extreme self-interest. It's named after Niccolo Machiavelli, from ideas he advocated in his well-known book, *The Prince*. You may remember it from school."

A few courtroom observers snickered.

Ruby turned to the prosecutor's table. "Your witness."

Assistant DA Samuel Webster got to his feet but did not approach the stand. "Dr. Jacobs, who reported that Vivien Lumi had conversations with her mirror?"

He looked at his notes. "Her stepdaughter, Bianca Lumi Regis."

"Anyone else?"

The psychiatrist re-examined his papers. "Doesn't appear so."

"No further questions."

The doctor stepped down and the next witness was sworn in.

Ruby cleared her throat. "May I approach the bench?"

The judge studied her for a moment. "You may."

"Your honor, I stipulate that this witness may prove to be hostile, given his divided loyalties between his late wife and his daughter."

"Noted."

Ruby moved close to the stand. "Would you state your name and your relationship to the deceased?"

"My name is Oscar Lumi. Vivien was my wife."

"She was the stepmother of Bianca Lumi Regis?"

"Yes."

"Please describe their relationship."

"Bianca was very attached to her mother. After she died…" he looked down at his hands. "After she died, I thought it would be best for Bianca to have a mother, so I remarried. Bianca never accepted Vivien. And Vivien, well, she took that very personally. She really did try, for a while. My wife was big on social media, so she posted a lot of photos of her and Bianca together. Everyone always said how beautiful Bianca was, and I think it made Vivien sad, because what was in the pictures and what was in real life were two very different things. After a while, she just gave up."

"Did you try to stop any of her attempts to get rid of your daughter?"

"What? Look… Vivien wanted Bianca out of the house when she turned 18. I love my daughter very much, but there was a lot of tension at home. It was almost unbearable. I admit that we moved her into an apartment for college on the first possible day. I hoped that just having some space would help things simmer down."

"Did you have a key to this apartment?"

"Yes. Vivien insisted on it. It was for security reasons. In case something happened, you know?"

Ruby glanced at the judge. "Mr. Lumi, who is Richard Devereaux?"

He closed his eyes for a moment and then looked up at the ceiling before answering. "He's an estate-planning attorney my wife hired."

"Did you know that Vivien planned to rob your daughter of her inheritance?"

"Objection!" Webster got to his feet. "That calls for speculation. Besides, Ms. Lawson is well aware that Mr. Lumi's assets were being put in trust to protect both him and his estate."

The judge nodded. "Sustained."

Ruby smirked. "I'll withdraw the question. I reserve the right to recall this witness later on in the proceedings."

"So stipulated. Mr. Webster?"

"No questions."

"I call Kevin Nguyen to the stand."

A pale and scrawny man made his way to the front of the courtroom and was sworn in.

"Mr. Nguyen, how do you know Bianca Lumi Regis?"

He yawned. "Sorry. I work nights. Been up almost twenty-four hours and I'm a little sleepy. Bianca cleans apartments for extra money. She does mine on Tuesdays."

"Would you describe the events of September second?"

"Sure. I had to run some errands before work, so I left way early. Bianca lives across from me, in 317. Gerald Martin from 320 was bouncing down the hall, coming home from his job—guess you'd be happy too, if you worked at a dispensary."

The bailiff chuckled.

"Mickey Aster from next-door was headed to the laundry room. I only noticed because he sneezed louder than air brakes on a bus and startled me. That's when I saw Bianca's door was ajar. We were all worried something happened to her, so we looked inside."

"Do you remember the time?"

"Five thirty-ish."

"And what did you find in the apartment?"

"Bianca was laying on the floor, tangled up in some kind of elasticated underthings. We called for an ambulance. They cut her out of that getup and she was fine. Paramedics said it was squeezing her too hard and also making her overheat. She passed out from it."

"And you submitted video from your doorbell camera to the police?"

"Yes."

"Your honor, I'd like to play the video clip from Mr. Nguyen's camera. This would be the first attempt the Vivien Lumi made on Bianca's life."

The judge nodded.

A large screen on the wall near the judge's bench flickered, then a recording of an older woman exiting the apartment 317 and walking out of frame played. Ruby replayed the footage, then paused when the woman's face was clearly visible.

"Mr. Nguyen, can you identify this woman?"

"Yeah. That's Bianca's stepmom. I'd met her before."

"Thank you. I'd also like to point out the timestamp on the video. Four fifty-two PM on September second. Your witness, Counselor."

The prosecutor stood. "Mr. Nguyen, when was the last time you saw Mrs. Lumi and her stepdaughter?"

"It was the day before we found Bianca on the floor. I was coming home a little later than usual, because I stopped for breakfast. Saw them at the parking garage elevator—they got out before I got in."

"How did Mrs. Lumi seem? Was she hostile? Angry?"

The witness looked up toward the ceiling and furrowed his brow. "She seemed nice enough. If there were any bad vibes, I don't remember it."

A young man at the prosecutor's table took notes.

"Thank you. No further questions." Samuel nodded to Mr. Nguyen.

Ruby flashed the prosecutor the barest hint of a smile. "I'd like to call my next witness, Jordan Adams."

When he was asked to tell the 'truth, the whole truth, and nothing but the truth,' he answered, "As much as I can."

The judge scowled. "That's a yes or no question, the answer to which is either 'I will' or 'I will not.' Pick one."

Jordan's eyes darted around the courtroom. "I-I will."

Ruby approached the witness stand. "It's alright, Jordan. You're perfectly safe here. I'd like you to describe the events on September eighth. With regard to Ms. Lumi Regis."

"It was exactly 14:00 hours. I was coming back from restocking my provisions. I came out of the stairwell—I don't trust the elevator—and saw the door to apartment 317 open and Miss Bianca lying partway in the corridor. Which was weird, because she'd cleaned my rooms that morning and didn't exhibit any unusual symptoms."

"And what did you do when you saw her?"

"I went to my apartment and called her next-door neighbor, Victor Hu. He works from home, so I figured he'd be there. He has bad anxiety, and he was just too bashful to touch her. He hung up and said he'd call her neighbor on the other side, Mr. Abner McClasky."

"And then what happened?"

"I watched through my doorbell camera and saw the old man come out. I could hear him grumping and grumbling, even through the door." Jordan shook his head. "He poked her with his cane, then leaned over her. Then she sat up, clutching at her throat. Apparently, she had a choker necklace on way too tight and blacked out."

"Thank you, Jordan. Your honor, I'd like to show another video clip from Mr. Nguyen's doorbell camera."

"Proceed."

Again, the screen flickered to life and an image of Vivien Lumi emerged from Bianca's apartment, put her phone to her ear, and walked out of sight.

"Your honor, please note the timestamp: September eight, one fifteen PM." Ruby took a few backward steps toward her table. "Thank you, Jordan."

He started to rise, and Samuel Webster jumped up. "Mr. Adams. I have a few questions for you." He stepped closer to the witness. "Why didn't you approach Ms. Lumi Regis yourself? Would you please explain?"

Jordan swallowed and his eyes flicked to Ruby. Her lips twitched before she looked away. He tugged at the collar of his button-down shirt. "I thought it might be a trap."

"A trap—one that you were happy to send Mr. Hu and Mr. McClasky into?"

"Oh, no, no, no." Jordan shook his head vigorously. "No, it wasn't dangerous for them."

"And why was that?"

"Well…" he leaned forward. "They're always watching me. And if I had been distracted and put my things down to try to help Miss Bianca, they might have been able to grab me. I mean, one could have transmogrified into a doppelganger of her. I don't like to think she was in on it but I can't be too careful."

"That's understandable. Who is it that you were worried would grab you?"

"I-I'd rather not say. How do I know there aren't any here in this room?"

"Mr. Adams, I think at this point, the cat's already out of the bag."

Jordan bowed his head and began to rock himself. He said something in a hoarse, incomprehensible whisper.

"I'm sorry. Could you repeat that?"

Without looking up, Jordan said, "The reptoids."

"And where do these reptoids come from?"

"Their planet orbits Mintaka, in Orion's belt."

"Thank you, Mr. Adams I have no further questions."

Ruby shot Samuel a withering look as he made his way back to his table. She'd known it was a risk calling Adams to the stand, but that video from Nguyer's front door couldn't be discredited by the dopey neighbor.

"I'd like to call Dr. Franco Calabasas to the stand."

He rose and was sworn in.

"Dr. Calabasas, are you familiar with both Mrs. Lumi and Mrs. Lumi Regis?"

"I am."

"Would you please tell the court what happened on October third?"

"Certainly! My office opens at nine, so at eight, I had stepped across the hall to see Mr. McClasky, as he was complaining of a sore back. While I was working on him, there came a terrible pounding on the wall, accompanied by gurgling and gasping. I ran to Bianca's door and it was locked, so I called Findlay Regis, the maintenance man."

"Findlay Regis, the defendant?"

The doctor sighed. "Yes. The defendant. He rushed down from the fourth floor. Upon hearing the wheezing and groaning, he immediately unlocked the door. We found Bianca semi-conscious on the kitchen floor. Half an apple lay next to her, so I deduced her to be choking. I shouted for Findlay to roll her onto her side, and when he did so, the offending fruit became dislodged. Bianca was so grateful she flung her arms around his neck and kissed him. I believe they eloped to Las Vegas that weekend."

Observers in the courtroom tittered, and even the severe judge cracked a momentary smile before banging the gavel and growling "Order!"

Ruby turned toward the judge. "Your honor—"

"Show the video."

As in the other clips, Vivien Lumi left Bianca's apartment, this time carrying a reuseable grocery bag. The timestamp was forty-five minutes before the doctor found Bianca.

Samuel Webster got to his feet. "Dr. Calabasas, it's very lucky for Bianca Lumi to have a trained medical professional just next-door when she needed help. For court records, where did you attend medical school?"

"Bendmora Chiropractic College."

Ruby pursed her lips. There he was again, trying to discredit her witnesses. Ah, well. It *was* his job. Let him try to discredit the video.

Samuel turned toward the judge. "No further questions, your honor."

Ruby set down the pen she'd been writing notes with. "Now I would like to call Bianca Lumi Regis to the stand."

Bianca wore a pale blue dress that matched the color of her eyes, although the pallor of her skin made the dark circles under her eyes stand out. A red bow decorated her black hair. As she took her oath, her voice was scarcely above a whisper, and she flinched like a hunted animal when the clerk knocked some papers to the floor.

"Mrs. Regis." Ruby handed her a tissue. "You believe your stepmother had been trying to cut you out of the family, and when that didn't work, she stalked and attacked you? She might very well have succeeded in murdering you, if not for Findlay and Dr. Calabasas. Would you say she was a clear and present threat?"

"Yes," Bianca answered between sniffles.

"Were you in fear for your life from her?"

"Definitely."

"Who could blame you? There's video evidence of her entering and leaving your apartment just before each of your three near-fatal mishaps."

Bianca nodded.

"I know this won't be easy for you, but would you describe what happened at your welcome home party when you got back from Las Vegas?"

"My best friend, Cindy, took care of Findlay's cat while we were out of town, so she had a key. She set up a whole surprise party for us when we walked in the door. There were, I think, twenty people there. We had a great time, until about nine-thirty."

"What happened then?"

"Vivien let herself into the apartment. I told Daddy to take away her key, but he always put her ahead of me." Bianca blotted her eyes. "Anyway, it got... awkward, and our friends all left. She... she came at me with the baseball bat Findlay keeps near the front door. It all happened so fast. He grabbed a pot of boiling water from the stove and threw it on her—she just wouldn't stop."

"That must have been terrifying."

"It was!" Bianca made a little sobbing hiccup. "But what happened next... she ran around in circles in the living room, screaming. Then she fell over. We called for an ambulance—hospital said it was a heart attack."

"Why was there water boiling on the stove during your party?"

"I was going to make a pitcher of tea." Bianca dabbed at her eyes.

Ruby handed her another tissue. "So, your stepmother, who has a history of making attempts on your life, tried to beat you with a baseball bat and your husband saved you with his quick thinking. Is that accurate?"

Bianca nodded. "Yes."

"This very unfortunate incident is a clear case of self-defense. I move for dismissal."

The door to the courtroom opened and a courier delivered a large manilla envelope to the prosecutor's table.

Samuel carried it to the judge and pulled three smaller manila envelopes out of it. "Your honor, before you rule on dismissal, I'd like to enter these documents into evidence.

Ruby hurried to the bench. The judge handed her one envelope, then removed the contents of another and thumbed through it before handing it to the clerk.

The prosecutor quirked an eyebrow. "I have some questions for your witness."

"I request an hour recess to review this new information to see how it may affect my client." Ruby tried not to sound too desperate.

"Denied. We're almost at the end of the day. I will, however, grant you fifteen minutes."

The bailiff strode into the courtroom. "All rise."

The observers got to their feet.

The judge took his place on the bench. "You may be seated. Prosecutor, your witness."

Samuel raised a computer printout. "Mrs. Regis. Your claim is that your stepmother barged into your party. However, once we finally obtained her phone records, we discovered that she received a call about thirty minutes to an hour before each of your, shall we say, near death experiences from a number that she had saved in her contacts list and named 'B Temp.' The phone from which the call was made is a pre-paid one, popularly known as a 'burner phone,' and each time, it pinged off the cell tower closest to your house. Do you have any explanation for that?"

"No, sir. I don't know anything about it."

Samuel's mouth tightened almost imperceptibly. "I see. Our office received an anonymous tip, and we subpoenaed security video and sales information from the Walmart near your house. Would you please identify the person in this photo?" he handed her an 11" x 17" blow up of a woman at the Walmart self-checkout.

Bianca's eyes darkened. "It's me."

"Thank you. Let the record state that Mrs. Regis identified herself as the person purchasing a pre-paid phone in this still image from checkout security video."

"Where did you get the Rohypnol?"

"What?" Bianca collapsed back in her chair. "I have no idea what you're talking about!"

Ruby paused. She could object, but if the DA was going after Bianca, she'd allow Samuel to do the heavy lifting and get her client off the hook. Didn't much matter to her whether Vivien or Bianca was the villain—her job was to defend Findlay, and now she had the option of arguing that he was protecting his home and family from a crazed stepmother, or that he was an innocent duped into a murder plot by a Machiavellian wife. The shadow of a doubt was getting wider.

"Mrs. Regis. The county medical examiner ruled the manner of Mrs. Lumi's death as a homicide, while the means was a heart attack, brought on by dousing her in boiling water, and declined to do a full autopsy, based on records from the hospital's emergency room. Your internet browser history shows that you researched whether Rohypnol overdose could be mistaken for a heart attack."

"You can't prove it was me," Bianca growled. "Findlay has just as much access to that computer as I did."

"Your father requested a full autopsy from a consulting pathologist and she put a rush on the toxicology screen. Your stepmother had enough roofie in her system to knock out three horses. The only place she could possibly have ingested it was at your apartment. Rohypnol takes effect in fifteen to twenty minutes. She could not have completed the thirty-minute trip from her house to your residence if she had taken it before she set out, or even in the parking lot before she came up, given the amount of time she was there before your other guests left."

Bianca covered her mouth with her hands, then began to wring them in her lap. "I told you she was mentally ill. She talked to a mirror for Pete's sake. Vivien probably just wanted to make us look bad by collapsing at our house. I wouldn't put it past her."

"And yet she relentlessly came at you with a bat?"

Bianca's eyes hardened and she clenched her jaw.

"Mrs. Regis, you and your friends, Cindy and Belle, attended the Halloween Bash at Club Venom on October seventh, did you not?"

"Yes."

"Given its reputation as a distribution hub, Club Venom has been the target of a drug trafficking investigation for several months. If you'd like, I can subpoena Chaco, the main dealer there, who's now awaiting trial on drug charges. I'm sure he'd be eager to cooperate for a reduced sentence."

Bianca fixed her angry eyes on her husband, seated at the defense table.

"Mrs. Regis, you were the only one who ever reported Vivien Lumi talking to her mirror. You did everything in your power to portray your stepmother as mentally unstable. On four separate occasions, you called her on your burner phone to lure her to your apartment so you could stage these alleged attacks, where you were found, pretending to be injured, shortly after she was recorded leaving your home on your neighbor's camera."

The witness shifted in her seat, looking for all the world like an angry tiger, ready to pounce. Ruby could almost feel Bianca's claws flexing.

Samuel took a step closer to the stand. "On the night of her death, either you or your husband roofied Vivien Lumi, then poured boiling water over her as part of your cover story for the murder that you planned well in advance. You eloped with Mr. Regis so that you couldn't be compelled to testify against each other. Which one of you slipped her the drugs before you murdered her?"

"I'm not gonna answer that." Her eyes cut to Ruby. "I know my rights."

Ruby glanced at her client. Just because a person cannot be *compelled* to testify against their spouse doesn't mean they aren't *allowed* to. Always better to be a cooperating witness than a co-defendant.

Samuel approached the bench. "Your honor, I move that this witness be bound over, pending murder charges."

The judge inclined his head toward Bianca. "Bailiff!"

Ruby nodded to Findlay. He wasn't completely off the hook—yet—but his chances were suddenly a great deal better, especially if *I can prove they weren't in it together.*

Hi ho, hi ho. It's off to work I go.

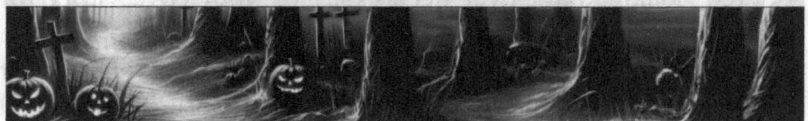

Dormant

By A.B. Richards

FELIPE wrinkled his nose. *Is that… gas?* He moved the bouquet of flowers closer to his face, but the noxious odor got stronger as he approached his date's front door. After matching on the dating app over a month ago, tonight—Friday—would be their first face-to-face meeting. He was already nervous, but the stench made his skin crawl.

He messaged her, "I'm here!" But after a full minute, it remained unread.

He rang the doorbell. There was no response.

The powerful smell of natural gas nearly drove him to panic. *Was Dawn all right? Not if she was inside that house.* He tried turning the knob, but it was locked. He dropped the flowers on the stoop and raced around to the back.

That door was also locked, so he grabbed a deck chair and smashed a window. The concentrated methane mix made him nauseous when he poked his head through the opening long enough to see an inert form lying on the floor in the hallway.

Padding his arm with a seat cushion, he broke out the rest of the glass and climbed through the window. Felipe rushed to open the back door wide and turn off the four cooktop burners that were unlit but set to high. Lightheaded, he stumbled down the hall and scooped the blonde woman up in his arms and hurried outside.

Once he made sure she was breathing, he called 9-1-1.

Sitting next to Dawn's hospital bed, Felipe gazed at her. The in-person Dawn was even better than her profile picture. Hair the color of sunflowers spread across her stark white pillow, highlighting the graceful curves of her face. She'd just fallen asleep, and he would need to go home soon to take care of Chip.

Thoughts about what happened buzzed in his brain like an angry bee. *One burner turned on could be an accident. All four? No way. Somebody did that.*

He shook his head. She knew exactly when he would arrive at her house and had seemed so excited about the meeting. Felipe couldn't, wouldn't, believe suicide was a possibility. If she had wanted to kill herself, she would have waited until she was sure nobody was coming to find her. *Right?*

The door opened silently, and two men in suits stepped inside.

Felipe looked up. "Hey, detectives." He'd given them a statement earlier.

"Mr. Rosa." The one he thought was called Blanchard nodded to him.

"How's the patient?" the other—Smith? Smits? Smythe?—asked.

"Better." Felipe kept his voice quiet. "She just went to sleep."

Blanchard frowned. "Bad timing. We really need to speak with her. I'm afraid we'll have to ask you to step out of the room."

Felipe's fingers brushed softly over Dawn's hand as he looked at the detectives. "Gotta go feed my dog, anyway." He turned back toward the patient. "I'll see you tomorrow. Sweet dreams," he whispered.

He paused outside the door and listened as the cops awakened Dawn and introduced themselves.

Blanchard said something Felipe couldn't quite hear, then, "Tell us what happened this afternoon."

"I don't know. I was getting ready for my date, then I woke up here."

Felipe smiled with relief as he walked down the hall and all the way out to the parking garage.

Chip stopped to sniff a mailbox post, and Felipe waved to his neighbor. "Hey, Dave! Halloween deco's looking good."

"Thanks! Did you notice the new one?" Dave gestured to a ragged figure dressed in black with tattered, cobwebby wings.

Felipe pushed the button on the leash to let out a little more of the nylon tape so Chip could stay at his post while his owner checked out the malignant fairy. As he approached, her eyes glowed green and her wings flapped. Even though he should have been expecting it, he jumped.

Chip raised his head and pricked his ears, then resumed reading the pee-mail.

"That's a good one. Looks very realistic. Where'd you get her?"

"Online."

"Where else, huh?"

Chip added his own reply to the message thread and wagged his tail.

"See ya, Dave."

Felipe and Chip strolled farther down the block. The house four doors down had a sixteen-foot black dragon with glowing purple eyes. Scutes on its underside and spikes on its back were an eerie, luminescent lavender. A chilly October breeze pushed the inflatable against its moorings, causing it to bob from side to side.

Chip pinned his ears and let out a low, rumbling growl.

Felipe tugged on the leash. "Come on, you silly dog. It's not real."

With three sharp barks, Chip followed, although he looked back every few steps to make sure the monster had heeded his warning to stay where it was.

They turned the corner, and the pup settled. Carolyn Rogers' home was exactly as he would have expected it. A stack of pastel and silver painted pumpkins decorated the front porch and a twig wreath with whimsical witches hung from the door.

Cute-core. Felipe sighed, and his thoughts wandered to Dawn. He'd always thought that 'love at first sight' was a ridiculous trope invented by Hollywood. But his heart had skipped a beat when he clicked on her profile and her magnificent violet eyes stared back at him. And when she opened them in the hospital and gazed deeply into his own, he just knew she was The One.

Chip and Felipe rounded the last corner, and the dog squatted for some solid waste disposal.

"Really? Here? Hurry up. If Mr. Hawkins sees you, he'll come out here to shout at us. Might even bring his gun." *Wouldn't be the first time.*

Felipe reached into his pocket for a bag.

Mr. Hawkins did not, in fact, see them, and the pair made it home without incident. As Chip wolfed down his dinner, Felipe opened his laptop and scoured the local news.

He'd known Dawn was an environmental compliance officer for the county. But he hadn't known that her report on Castle Manufacturing sparked the biggest illegal chemical release fine, plus cleanup costs, of any company in the history of the entire state. *Could that be related to the attempt on her life?*

First, he found a video of an interview with her two elderly aunts, Florinda and Fani, who'd been by to drop off a bag of vegetables from their garden the day of the incident.

Yet another clip showed her tearful landlady, Millicent Specter, clutching a skein of green yarn. "Dawn was trying to teach herself to knit. For some odd reason, my cousin bought *me* hand-spun, hand-dyed yarn from her trip to Colorado. It's beautiful, but what was I going to do with it? I brought it over for Dawn, but when she didn't come to the door, I just assumed she wasn't home. Must have missed that young fella who pulled her outta the house by mere minutes."

So, who dunnit? The aunts? The landlady? Someone from Castle Manufacturing? That was a problem for the police. He, however, took it upon himself to keep her safe.

Felipe spent a sizeable chunk of Saturday at the hospital with Dawn. Her aunties also visited for a while. Dawn was feeling much better, and after she grew weary from talking, Fani and Florinda left. Felipe used his phone to read her stories from the internet until the doctor came in.

As long as she continued to improve at the current rate, she could go home tomorrow afternoon.

On Sunday, the aunties cooked a meal and arranged a large vase of flowers while Felipe fetched Dawn from the hospital. After stuffing themselves with delicious food, they moved to the living room and put on a movie. On the couch, Dawn nestled under Felipe's protective arm, while the aunts huddled next to each other on the loveseat.

As the credits rolled, Fani nudged her sister with an elbow while smiling coyly at Dawn. "It'll be dark soon, and you know Florinda doesn't drive at night. We'd best be going."

Puzzlement crinkled Florinda's face for a moment before her eyes opened wide and a smile lit her face. "Yes. Must be going. Have a wonderful evening, you two."

Almost as a unit, the women rose and picked up their purses.

Felipe leaned forward to stand.

"No, no. Don't get up. We know the way out." Fani patted him on the shoulder. She stooped to kiss her niece on the top of her head. "Don't worry about that casserole dish, dear. I'll pick it up later."

Felipe felt a prick of guilt as his watch vibrated, signaling doggie dinner time. Knowing he'd be out most of the day and may not make the feeding schedule, Felipe had left Chip at his sister's house. Dawn had told him she loved animals and couldn't wait to meet the doggo. He only hoped the pup was as smitten with her as he was.

"So." Dawn intertwined her fingers with Felipe's. "How are we going to keep ourselves entertained this evening?"

"Uh… we could play cards?"

"Not exactly what I had in mind."

"Oh."

She rested her hand on his thigh.

"Oh!" His eyes opened wide. "Are you sure? You just got out of the hospital."

She stretched up to kiss him. Electricity tingled through Felipe's skin, and his hands trembled as he reached for her.

The back doorknob rattled. Felipe leaped to his feet. "What was that?"

"Someone's trying to get in!"

He dialed 91 and handed her his phone. "You stay here. If you see anyone or hear me shout, hit the last 1."

Dawn nodded.

Felipe scrambled to the kitchen, turning on every light in his path. He drew the biggest knife from the butcher block and snapped on the exterior light as he opened the back door. A dark figure ran for the open gate. He gave chase, but it disappeared down the brushy utility easement not far from Dawn's house. Aware of the darkness that lurked in the hearts of some people, Felipe feared to leave her unprotected and sprinted back down the sidewalk.

When he returned to the living room, Dawn flung herself into his arms.

He held her for a while, then said, "Didn't see who it was. Maybe we should go to my house?"

"I'd feel safer there. I'll call Detective Blanchard on the way."

After that, she made a single trip to her own place to collect her clothes. Much to her landlady's consternation, she soon sublet the home to one of her friends, who was going through a nasty breakup. Within two short months, Dawn found she was pregnant. With twins.

Shortly after that, the friend subleasing the house discovered her brakes had been tampered with, and, after a difficult day downtown in an interrogation room, Millicent Specter confessed to trying to kill both Dawn and her friend. She had learned she could get almost triple what she was charging Dawn for rent and was desperate to squirm out of the long-term lease she'd signed with her. The night she was bailed out, the news reported that she had laid down on a train track and that was that.

It wasn't until the kids—fraternal twins, a boy called Albert, and a girl named Eileen—were in preschool that the scratching started. Dawn and Felipe had arranged their work schedules so that she dropped off and he picked up.

The shorter, chillier October days brought sweaters out of closets. One afternoon, as Felipe pulled into a parking space, he noticed her.

Long blonde hair.

Pink sweater with fluff at the cuffs and hem.

Ugg suede boots.

So much like Cecily. He closed his eyes, remembering. She'd been his first. Her hair was the softest thing he'd ever touched and smelled of flowers and spice. Felipe breathed deeply, letting images from the past float around him in an intoxicating pool. And that's when the scratching started. A noise inside his head. Something locked away, trying to get out.

A slamming car door smashed his reverie. His hand jerked toward the keys, and he hurried into the building to pick up his children. Once he got to the classroom, a grin split his face. His kids grabbed their backpacks and ran to him.

Felipe hugged them both, then tilted his head in the direction of a little girl in a red jacket clinging to the blonde in the pink sweater. "Who's that? Is she one of your friends?"

Ted nodded "Her is Lizzie. We do puzzles."

"Maybe you should invite her over to play sometime."

"Yay!" Eileen twirled around, nearly smacking her father in the nose with her tiny backpack.

Lizzie and her mom passed by, and Felipe inhaled deeply, hoping to catch the scent of her perfume. No such luck. He signed the kids out and took them home.

He could not fall asleep that night. Dawn's slow, deep breathing began to get on his nerves, plucking each tense strand until it was angry and sore. With a huff, he whipped off his covers and stalked out of the room. Chip did not follow him. He'd become Dawn's shadow over the past few days. *Ungrateful mutt.*

Felipe snapped open the lock and strode out onto the patio. Moonlight kissed the whiskey barrel of mums by the door, washing out the bright colors to a ghostly grey. He paced from the top-of-the line outdoor kitchen on one end to the lounging area at the other until the frigid air cooled his inflamed nerves.

Felipe sat on the outdoor sectional and stared up at the silvery orb in the sky. He had a good life, he and Dawn. Her job paid well, and while his base salary was only average, he brought in a crazy amount of overtime pay installing home security systems on the weekends. The kids were amazing. And he loved Dawn a thousand times more now than the day they'd met.

And yet the scratching got louder.

He had a good thing going, and nobody with a shred of sense would risk losing everything. Plenty of people would kill for his life. But he stood in front of the locked door inside his head, listening to the frantic scraping of claws on metaphorical steel. Felipe shook himself and slouched into the house, where he turned on the TV and flipped through the channels until his thumb slowed and he fell asleep.

Felipe and Lizzie's mom were parked next to each other, loading children into car seats at the same time. He got Albert strapped in and moved around the vehicle to buckle Eileen. Lizzie's mom had just closed the door.

"Hi! I'm Felipe. My kids are always talking about playing with Lizzie at school, and my wife wanted me to ask if you'd like to bring them for a play date."

The blonde cocked her head and slowly stepped back. "Um. Yeah, I guess. Why don't you write down her number, and I'll get in touch. Perhaps we could go to the park or something. What's her name?"

"Dawn."

He pulled the hardware store receipt from his pocket. "Hold on, let me find a pen."

It only took a moment for him to locate one in the center console. He wrote his wife's contact info, along with 'Eileen and Albert's mom from preschool.' Felipe handed her the slip of paper.

"Okay. Thanks." She hurried to the other side of her car and got in, not even telling him her name.

It hadn't gone as well as he had hoped. He was sure they'd exchange names and numbers. Without a name, it would be difficult to find out more about her. He'd just call her Cecily II for now. Felipe finished securing Eileen and started for home. So absorbed in his memory of the time he had given Cecily a bubble bath, he almost ran a red light. Baths were a special activity he did with all his girls, but as the first, she'd been the most memorable.

The best thing about school days was that the kids were so tired they often fell asleep before Felipe finished their bedtime story. Once their eyes shut, he stopped reading and waited a minute or two for complaints. When none came, he closed the book of fairy tales and crept out of the room. Felipe hurried downstairs to find Dawn frowning at her phone.

"What's wrong?"

"Some rando named Hailey is texting me about going to the park. I'll just block—"

"No! That's…" Took a second to remember the kid's name. "Lizzie's mom. From school? She said Lizzie won't shut up about Albert and Eileen, and she wanted to make a play date."

"Oh. That makes sense, then. I'll see if they want to go trick-or-treating with us this weekend."

Eileen's black cat ears tilted haphazardly on her head, while Albert's pumpkin top beret had been lost almost immediately after trick-or-treating had commenced. The route may have been a little ambitious—all three kids were too tired to walk before they got back to Lizzie's house. Felipe carried the drowsy tots from the car into their own living room. Dawn brought up the rear with their candy bags.

She set them on the floor by the children. "Two pieces, then it's time to brush teeth and put on jim-jams."

The toddlers, who had stretched out on the rug and propped their heads on their hands because they were too tired to sit up, complained about having to go to bed as they picked through the sugary morsels.

Dawn sat next to Felipe on the loveseat. "I'm glad you gave Hailey my number. She and Matt seem like a lot of fun."

Felipe blinked. *Hailey? Oh! Cecily II.* "Yeah. It was interesting to see a different neighborhood for T-O-T."

The kids were soon a-snooze and Felipe brought in glasses of wine to the living room. Dawn took one, and they snuggled on the couch together with the TV on.

After a few minutes, she yawned. "Babe? What kind of wine is this?"

"Malbec. Why?"

"How long has it been open? It tastes a little vinegary."

"Probably because you ate candy right before you drank some."

Dawn shrugged and set her glass on the coffee table. "Hmmm."

As he stroked her hair, he unlocked the metal door in his head and peered into the darkness. At first, all was still, then a foul and shaggy thing came bounding out.

The Bathtub Killer was no longer dormant.

He smiled and carefully laid a drowsy Dawn on the couch as he slipped away.

In the garage, he gathered the duct tape, bubble bath, and bleach he'd purchased earlier in the week, then fumbled for his keys. He knew where Cecily II lived now. His plan was to bind Matt's hands and tape the plastic shopping bag over his head while he was asleep. Then Felipe would take his time with Cecily II. He was so excited he could hardly breathe as the jointed door rolled open.

Feet. Legs. Hips. Who on earth was standing out there?

"Why did you put sleeping pills in my wine, Felipe?" Dawn, or something resembling her, stepped into the garage. Her eyes glowed green and her skin was... wrong.

Her face and bare arms glittered like scales as she passed through the sallow light from the overhead door opener. Thoughts of Cecily II drained away, water through Felipe's fingers. He scooted backward until he hit the wall.

Dawn was up against him faster than he could think. She smacked the button, and the garage door began to groan closed behind her.

Her lips against his ear, she murmured, "Never mind. I know why." She traced his cheek from the edge of his eye to the corner of his mouth with a dagger-sharp claw.

Felipe struggled to say something as blood oozed down his face, but all he could manage was a liquidy gurgle. *When had her teeth gotten so pointed?*

Dawn laughed. "I'm glad I didn't kill you that first day—I fully intended to. But you know what? It was a good thing that Mrs. Specter thwarted my plans. Albert and Eileen are the best part of my life."

"Wh-what about me?" Felipe squeaked, suddenly feeling a twinge of guilt about leaving the old woman unconscious on the rail line.

"You, my darling, you have been a nice pet. But Mother always did tell me not to play with my food."

Not Worth Beans
By A.B. Richards

JACKIE rang the doorbell. When the door swung open, a grinning, hairy man with a ponderous beer gut stood in the entry.

Naked.

Handing over the food with a grimace, Jackie said, "Enjoy your meal."

The man laughed, his belly jiggling like tofu in a blender.

Where's the eye bleach when you need it? Jackie power-walked to his battered Camry, got inside, and locked his doors. He opened the delivery app and blocked the customer. He didn't get paid nearly enough for that.

Most people just wanted their dinner and weren't interested in messing with the driver, but every so often… he shook his head as he put the car in gear and pulled away from the curb. He hated to think of what might have happened if he had been female.

At least the nude dude had offered a big tip. Jackie and his mom might be able to pay the mortgage this month, after all. All he needed were a few more deliveries, especially if they had 20% tips or better.

But that would have to wait until this evening. At the moment, he had to lean on the gas to get to his class at the community college on time.

"What time did you say he'd be there, Mom?" Jackie scowled at his app. While he was in class, the weenie wagger had zeroed out his tip. Now he would have to do extra runs to make up for it.

"He said 6:30."

"And what was the price?"

"It was $125, firm. He'll be driving a green F150."

"Alright. I'm headin' out. May work late, so don't wait up."

"Thanks for taking care of this, Jackie."

He picked up the ceramic cow from the mantle and eased her into a pocket on his cargo pants. Jackie was sorry to see Moobelle go. As a little kid, he'd been obsessed with the antique, often sneaking her into his room. He had played games with her, and sometimes asked his mother to set a plate for her at dinner. Moobelle had been an imaginary friend who wasn't entirely imaginary.

She had humored him, probably because working two jobs didn't leave her much time or energy to entertain an energetic toddler. She'd let him run himself ragged dancing circles around the figurine and trying to impress the porcelain bovine with any number of variations on cartwheels and somersaults.

They'd been selling off their possessions for some time now, and Moobelle was one of the few things of any value left. He hated to see her go, but hated the idea of living on the street even more.

As he drove to the grocery store, he tried to remember what it was that had made her so special. She didn't move or make noise. Perhaps it was because she had been his grandmother's and was a hazy link to his missing father.

The police had only done a cursory investigation, saying that he'd most likely left of his own accord. Asshole move, but not illegal. Jackie's mom was just as sure that something had happened to him. Jackie clung to that possibility. Otherwise, it meant that his father had abandoned him intentionally.

The low fuel light flashed on as Jackie pulled into a parking space at the grocery store. At least Moobelle's buyer was paying in cash. He could drive across the lot and get a splash of gas.

Jackie had arrived a few minutes early on purpose. He stood near the cart area in front of the grocery store under the concrete awning, where he could be out of the brisk October wind. He squinted into the fading light, scanning the parking area for green trucks. A small heap of bedraggled pumpkins nearby was marked 60% off. A woman with three costumed kids in tow gave him a sidelong glance as she hurried into the store.

Is it Halloween tonight? Ugh. I could be making so many *deliveries instead of standing here like an idiot. Pre- trick-or-treat food delivery—especially pizza—is a gold mine. This bro better show.*

At 6:28, a forest green, late-model pickup turned off the busy road into the parking area. The spotless truck slipped into a space only a few over from Jackie's primer-spotted Camry.

A man about Jackie's height got out and clicked the remote. The vehicle chirped and the side mirrors folded in.

Jackie shifted his weight. His passenger side mirror folded in when he stopped, but that was because one end of the duct tape had come unstuck.

The buyer adjusted his black hoodie and strode toward the grocery store. Jackie was mesmerized by the shimmering blue-grey hide of whatever exotic animal had lost its skin to the man's roach-killer boots.

When the man was close enough, Jackie cleared his throat. "Excuse me. Are you Mr. Smith?"

"Do you have the cow?" He did not pull back his hood.

"Yes." Jackie tugged the Velcro on his pocket and retrieved Moobelle.

Mr. Smith pulled his hands out of his own pockets and took her from Jackie. He turned her over, side to side, top to bottom, then raised her to his ear and gave her a shake.

"Hey! What are you doing?"

He handed Moobelle back, but before Jackie's fingers closed around the cow, Mr. Smith let go.

Moobelle dropped to the concrete and broke into several large pieces. Some dark ovals bounced off the pavement and rolled into the shards. *Had they come out of Moobelle, or from the man's hands?*

Jackie stood gaping at the destruction. *Are those… beans? Why would he do that?*

"Well, obviously, I don't want it now." Mr. Smith turned to leave.

"You did that deliberately!" Jackie snapped. "What is wrong with you?"

The man kept walking, but twisted his head and spoke over his shoulder. "Maybe you ought to clean that mess up and take it home with you." He chuckled. "Try planting some of those. Who knows what they were smuggling inside that cow?"

Still in shock and not knowing what else to do, Jackie trotted into the store and snatched a paper sack from one of the self-check stations. He placed the larger pieces in the bag, then used some cart wipes to push in the small fragments and beans. He just hoped no one he knew passed by—he was already humiliated enough.

Jackie's mother dashed out of the kitchen when he came through the door, a huge smile on her face. "Did you get the money?"

He raised the paper sack. "No. He broke her."

"What?" His mom dropped to the couch and rubbed her forehead. When she looked up, her eyelashes glistened with moisture. "I don't know how I'm going to pay the light bill now. They're gonna shut off the power tomorrow."

"How much do you need?"

"Ninety-eight dollars."

"I'll give you the money I've been saving for the mortgage. Planned to get it to you tomorrow, anyway." *'Cuz I don't have quite enough today.* "Pay the lights out of that. I'll just have to do some extra deliveries. That's all."

His mother hung her head. "I don't know what else to do."

He gave her a resolute smile. "It's alright, Mom. Once I get my degree, we'll be okay." *At the rate I'm going, I'll be forty by the time I graduate.*

"I only wish your father—"

"Mom. Don't."

Her lips pressed into a tight line, and she rose. "Guess I'll go finish up the dishes."

"Mom… do you know if Moobelle was filled with beans?"

Her brow furrowed,, and she moved to where Jackie stood. "Beans? Not that I'm aware of."

He opened the bag. Nestled amongst the broken pieces of china were a bunch of greenish blue beans. Jackie sighed. He was clearly much more tired than he thought. It seemed for a moment that they had a faint glow.

"Eww! They look moldy. Normal beans are not that color. I don't want these nasty things in my house!" She snatched the bag and hurried to the back door.

By the time Jackie realized what she was going to do, she'd already scattered a heaping handful into the grass.

"Stop! You're gonna cut yourself. Give me that—I'll take care of it."

"Fine. I have to go to work, anyway." She shoved the paper sack at him and strode inside.

Jackie spent his evening gluing Moobelle back together. There were a few small pieces missing, but Moobelle looked mostly like her old self when he was done.

A loud crack shattered Jackie's sleep.

He rolled off his mattress and onto the floor as a twisted black vine snaked through the broken glass of his window. He tried to scamper away on all fours, but a tendril shot out and wrapped itself around his ankles. With nothing to cling to, Jackie could do little more than cover his face as the vine yanked him feet-first through the shattered window, slamming his knee hard against the wooden frame.

Jackie thudded to the patchy grass of his backyard and struggled against the inexorable pull of the vine. He shook his head, struggling to figure out what he was seeing. He was being dragged toward something that looked like a gnarled old tree. Only it was all black, with thin, sparse twining branches sprouting at intervals along the trunk. The fact that it flickered and glitched in and out of existence made his brain question what his eyes were showing him.

More concerningly, what would happen when his feet hit it? Would they go right through, or shatter against the solid bore? Or was it just a dream, and he'd wake up and shake his head at the craziness of it?

Jackie didn't have long to wait. He braced for impact as best he could and squeezed his eyes shut.

And then everything stopped.

He blinked several times, hoping each time his lids opened, he would be safe on the mattress in his bedroom. Instead, he found himself inside a shallow cave. Outside, a dingy twilight swamped the trunks of enormous trees, and grey mist pooled at their feet. The silhouette of a castle loomed in the distance.

Where the Kentucky-fried hell am I?

He stood up, the cuts and scrapes from being dragged across the yard only now beginning to sting and throb. Jackie shook the grass and sand out of his boxers, one leg at a time. He suspected the tee shirt was ruined. Oh, well—it had been pretty threadbare to start with. He crept to the cave entrance and peered out.

Unseen in the forest that spread out before him, night creatures clicked, groaned, and snorted. Jackie craned his head to see the tops of the trees that scratched the belly of the gloomy sky, and they reminded him of pictures he'd seen of giant Sequoias in California.

Jackie returned to the cave and began running his hands along the walls, hoping to find an exit. He wanted no part of whatever was out there. On the back wall, his hand slipped through an invisible opening, but it was only large enough for his forearm. After he pulled it out, he couldn't find the hole again.

A few pebbles fell on his head. He stepped back and looked up. The roof of the cave was pale, but he was unable to tell any more than that. *Was it about to collapse?*

Jackie should have run. But he stood too long, listening, trying to identify the sounds he was hearing. Like claws scraping on stone, with a chitinous clicking over the top of it.

Another shower of sand and pebbles. Jackie cast his eyes up and found the white on the ceiling was flowing down the wall. His brain told him to flee, but his feet stayed glued to the floor.

The pale thing rippled across the rock and stopped a couple of yards away. The centipede-like creature reared off the ground, its countless legs waving as it pulled itself up, towering over Jackie. It wasn't until it started spitting acid at him that his body unfroze, and he fled. He'd dodged most of the spray, but his sleeve had been hit. He ripped off the shirt as he sprinted away and flung it into the woods.

Jackie was fast, but the centipede was gaining. He lurched between a narrow gap in a copse of smaller trees, hoping the monster was too wide. It barely slowed as it wound its body up a fat trunk and easily passed through sideways.

Jackie ran until he couldn't suck in enough air for his muscles to function. He was so dizzy he nearly fell as he stumbled over the rough ground. Then he tripped over a root and sprawled on the forest floor. Chest heaving, he rolled onto his back.

The centipede stopped. It raised up, twitched its antennae, and rotated its head a few times, then turned and sped off into the dark.

Shit. I don't want to know what that thing's scared of.

He struggled to silence his gasping and crawled into a patch of bracken at the base of a giant tree.

Shrubs rustled and rotting leaves crunched off to Jackie's left. A green snake as wide as a pickup truck slithered through the bushes. It paused near Jackie, raising its head and tasting the air with its tongue.

Jackie clamped his hand over his mouth to stop himself from screaming. The snake turned its head from one side to the other a few times, then continued along the centipede's path.

When he was certain the serpent was gone, Jackie got to his feet. He braced one arm against the nearest trunk to support his wobbly knees.

And snatched it away.

He hadn't expected the dark red bark to be damp and sticky. But it was the throbbing pulse of the tree that turned his blood to ice.

Now what? I have no idea how to get to the path, much less back home. Why is this happening to me?

He allowed himself to wallow in despair for a few moments. But if he wanted to find a way out, blubbering in the woods wasn't going to get him anywhere. Jackie would be an easy meal for one of these colossal creatures if he didn't pull himself together.

He might be, anyway.

"Oh, you poor dear thing."

Jackie spun around. He'd been so caught up in his pity party that he hadn't heard the woman come up behind him.

She was at least twice his height, wearing a pale blue apron over a full striped skirt. Before he could say anything, she lifted him to her hip and carried him like a toddler. He lacked the strength to resist, so he allowed himself to be hauled along. He may have to run from her later, but for now, it was a needed respite.

"It's dangerous for the wee folk out here. And you look a bit the worse for wear."

"What is this place? How did I get here? Who are you?"

Tsk. "Well, a 'thank you' for saving your skin might be nice."

"Sorry. Sorry. Thank you."

"You're welcome. You have found your way to the grounds of Canavalia Castle. It's been in my husband's family for... as long as anyone alive or dead remembers."

"O... kay." Jackie noticed that the pockets of her apron bulged with mushrooms. Some of them were as big as his head.

"Have lunch with me. I'll explain as best I can. My husband has shut himself away in his laboratory so much lately, and I would love to have a chat with someone."

Laboratory? Is he a mad scientist? "Oh. What is he working on?"

"That he guards like a dragon hoarding gold. They're quite the problem if you go up into the mountains, just so you know. Whatever he's doing, sometimes wee folk get pulled across the border into this place."

"So, I'm not the first."

"Far from it."

"And the others? Have they made it home?"

The woman pushed a limb out of her way and ducked under it. "Some of them."

Only some? "What happened to them?" Eyeing his blistered shoulder, he suspected he already knew the answer.

"It's a bit complicated, isn't it?"

"Sounds like it." Jackie licked his dry lips. "My name's Jackie. What should I call you?"

She paused. "He won't approve. But I'll tell you, anyway. Cirrina. You can call me Cirrina."

And with that, she stepped out of the trees and onto the path. The somber grey castle rose ahead of them.

Lush flower and vegetable beds lay ahead in the gap between the forest and the stone structure. The thing that most caught Jackie's eye was a teepee made of sticks and covered in blue vines. Among the azure leaves, dark red bean pods drooped like deflated sausages. Small, dark flowers sprouted from the vines and emitted a sickly sweet fragrance.

Beyond that, black chickens the size of Great Danes scratched and pecked in the yard, until they noticed Cirrina and flocked to her. As the inky birds crowded around their owner, a few of them squawked when they got their curved ram's horns briefly tangled. A jump here and a flap there freed them.

Jackie swallowed and looked more closely. *Wait. Chickens don't normally have horns, do they?* Their gleaming eyes were a disturbing shade of russet.

Cirrina gently shooed the birds away. "Go on! You've had your breakfast already."

Jackie had no idea what normal chickens ate, much less these freakish feathered fiends. He hoped they weren't carnivorous.

She set him down when she reached the portcullis. Unseen chains rattled and groaned as they lifted the massive wood and iron grate.

"C'mon, then, little man." Cirrina swept into the castle, the heavy wooden door opening as if by magic when she neared it. Jackie had to jog to keep up.

Dismay washed over him when they came to a spiral staircase. The risers were close to two feet tall, and his legs were still shaking after his race from the centipede.

"A bit steep for you, eh?" Not waiting for him to answer, she lifted him back up and set him on her hip.

I am not a toddler! But Jackie knew those stairs were more than a match for him in his current state.

At the top of the stairs, she put Jackie down and opened a hallway closet. She hummed to herself as she rummaged among the boxes and containers. At last, she picked up a crate and backed into the hall.

"I reckon it's a bit chilly in nothing but your skivvies. These are some clothes from when our son was a wee lad—might be something in here you can wear." She pulled out a pair of elastic-waist jeans and a plaid flannel shirt that had buttons sewn over snaps. "Try these."

Oh, wow. Cast-off baby clothes? But he had to admit he was cold. The pants were a little big, and the shirt was a little snug, but they were better than running around in nothing but ragged boxers. He hoped there were no mirrors nearby.

Hopping down the stairs as quickly as he could go, Jackie trailed behind Cirrina on the way to the kitchen, where they sat at the table chatting over cookies—that tasted of sugar-coated grass clippings—and tea that seemed to have been brewed from licorice and hot sauce. Still, it was like meeting a long-lost grandmother. Somehow, she drew Jackie's life story out of him, even though he usually kept it tightly under wraps.

Cirrina pulled a gold chain from under the collar of her dress and draped it around his neck. She had to cross it and loop it back several times so that he didn't trip over it. His shoulders sagged—it must have weighed four or five pounds.

"I'll wager you can get a few coins for that when you get home."

"If I get home." Jackie sighed.

"That grotto my husband built seems to be the place where your kind comes and goes here. I know the portal isn't stable, but if you're there waiting, you might be able to catch it when it opens."

"Easy for you to say. You aren't snack-sized."

Cirrina laughed softly. "If you stay on the path—"

A heavy wooden door somewhere inside the castle slammed shut.

"My husband!" Cirrina hissed. She grabbed Jackie's arm and hustled him into the pantry, holding up her finger to her lips.

Through the cracked door, Jackie watched Cirrina greet a man even taller than her. His thick black hair needed a trim, and stubble was scattered over his chin, but there was nothing unusual about him, aside from being twelve feet tall.

"Loligo, my darling! How has your work been today?"

He grunted. "Fine." Then he turned toward the pantry, raising his head and sniffing the air. "I smell a runt."

"I don't smell anything. You sure it isn't fumes from whatever you've been doing in the laboratory?"

He scowled and pulled a chair out from the table. "What's for lunch?"

Cirrina donned oven mitts and retrieved a plate from somewhere Jackie couldn't see from his limited line of sight. He didn't recognize a thing on the platter. The food was all the wrong color, all the wrong shape. Jackie breathed through his mouth as the pungent reek of sulfur made him want to gag. He put his hands on his stomach, wondering what had been in the cookies.

Jackie tried to take a step back to reduce his exposure to the noxious food smells, but his foot hit something. He froze, almost losing his balance. He turned to look at what had nearly blown his cover and spied a wicker basket filled with double-sized eggs. Jackie looked closer. Double-sized *golden* eggs. He considered slipping one into his pocket, but he was fresh out of them. *Damned baby clothes.*

After what seemed like hours, Loligo pushed his mostly empty plate away and rose. "Time to go back to work."

A short time later, the door slammed again.

Cirrina jerked open the pantry door. "Come! Hurry!"

She snatched him up and carried him under her arm like a loaf of bread until they were in the front courtyard. Cirrina whistled. The mob of black chickens parted.

From around the corner, a bird at least a foot taller than the others emerged.

This must be the big daddy chicken.

His scaly legs had a bigger girth than Jackie's waist, ending in thick, clawed feet. Spikes of red flesh rose from the top of its beak to the base of its obsidian horns.

Cirrina leaned over and whispered something to the bird, then lifted Jackie onto its muscular back. "Go!"

Jackie nearly fell as the chicken took off. Flailing, he grabbed its horns as the bird raced out of the yard and down the forest path.

When they arrived at the grotto. Jackie slid off the bird's back and patted its wing. "Thanks. Mr. Chicken. Hope you're not going to eat me."

The bird stationed itself in the entrance, facing the misty woods. Exhausted, Jackie leaned against the back of the cavern.

"Ahhh!" The sensation of falling ripped Jackie out of sleep. He landed in the grass with a thud.

Home! I'm home!

The patio door was locked, so he had to clamber back through his broken window. He stuffed the gold chain in his underwear drawer and shucked off the borrowed baby clothes, exchanging them for his own.

Mom must be worried sick. I'll go tell her—

The alarm on his phone began to buzz and chirp. His brow furrowed as he turned it off. It was 8:00 AM. On the same day, he got dragged into the grotto at Canavalia Castle. He knew it couldn't have happened long before his alarm—it was already getting light when he'd been yanked through the window. *How could this be? I was there most of the day.*

Jackie tip-toed to the kitchen. His mother looked up from spreading margarine on toast. "Hey." She gave him a tired smile. "Look, I'm sorry about being short with you last night. I'm exhausted, and so stressed about the bills. I didn't mean—"

"Mom, it's okay. Listen, did you hear glass breaking this morning? My window is shattered."

"What?" She set down the knife and hurried past him to his room.

He crossed the threshold a moment later. Hands on hips, she stood shaking her head. "Probably some jerk firing a gun in the air. Or rotten kids playing a dirty Halloween trick."

Jackie nodded. "Yeah. Guess that's it. I think there's some plywood in the garage. I'll go look."

As he searched through the dusty scrap lumber, he decided that thicker was better where plywood was concerned. Hopefully, the vine wouldn't come back, and if it did, perhaps it couldn't get through the three-quarter inch sheet. He found an assortment of wood screws and used the drill to put up the plywood. There was a one-inch gap at the bottom, so he duct-taped a trash bag over the makeshift repair.

When he came back inside, his mother had already left for her first job. He got busy on his phone, looking for the best place to sell gold. Too fancy, and they would question where he acquired that massive chain. Too low-rent, and they wouldn't give him enough. At last, he settled on a store and gathered the necklace into a pillowcase.

After his excursion to the Gold and Diamond Super Exchange, he was not set for life, but he was able to pay off the mortgage, catch up on the bills, and get a new-to-him car. When his mom asked where the money came from, he told her he'd lucked out on a scratch ticket.

Even though the economic pressure had eased, thoughts of those golden eggs in the basket danced in Jackie's head. One or two of those would put him through college, at least, and possibly grad school. He had no way of knowing if or when the vine would return, so he purchased a motion detector that sent an alert to his phone if it sensed movement.

Two weeks later, it pinged him. He had just gotten out of the shower and as soon as he saw the message, Jackie scrambled into his clothes and hurried into the backyard.

Sure enough, there was the twisted stalk, a scraggly vine probing the new plexiglass window to his room. The moment he came within range, it whipped toward him and wrapped around his left wrist. He stretched out his arm and allowed it to drag him into the grotto.

Jackie found Cirrina feeding her strange hens in the court-yard, and again she invited him inside for tea. She seemed delighted by having orchestrated his change of fortune and showed him the golden eggs.

"Take as many as you like, little man. My girls lay more every day."

The distant door slammed, and Cirrina shoved Jackie and the basket into the pantry.

"Gaw! What is that smell?" Loligo waved his meaty hand in front of his nose before sitting with his back to the pantry door.

"I'm afraid it's your lab coat, my love." Cirrina approached the table with a plate of stinking food.

Some green thing squirmed and wriggled in a beige sauce. Cirrina set the dish before Loligo and took a seat opposite her spouse.

Jackie clamped a hand over his mouth to stifle his gagging. He nearly lost it when the green thing screamed as Loligo leaned his head back and dropped it into his open jaws. Wet squelching noises followed. Jackie tried to force his brain to think about something, anything else, as he stuffed his pockets with the golden eggs. There was only room for five. But that should be more than enough.

After Loligo returned to his lab, Jackie again rode the black rooster to the grotto, where he leaned against the wall, visions of high-paying jobs dancing in his head, until he fell through it.

Smug, he got to his feet and dusted himself off. He was halfway to the patio door when one of the eggs in his pocket moved. Then another. He froze. *Are they hatching? How am I going to explain a brood of Hellchicks? Probably better to just crush them before they come out. No telling what kind of damage they'll do. The golden shells should still be fine to sell.* He spotted a brick lying near the downspout and picked it up.

As he pulled each egg out of his pockets, he was distraught to see that they'd turned an oily bronze. *Why did she lie to me?* He lined the squirming eggs up, more intent than ever on smashing them.

The first egg cracked open. Instead of a fluffy black chick, armored worms wriggled out. Jackie dropped the brick, too stunned to act. The rest of the eggs broke, and dozens of slimy creatures twisted out and onto the ground.

They were not large, perhaps three inches. The bony segments of their bodies clicked as they writhed and wiggled—they sounded like a crowd of people snapping. The grotesque worms looked eerily akin to skeleton human fingers, but with too many joints. Jackie fought the urge to scream and run into the house.

The little creepers began burrowing into the ground. He groped for the brick. By the time it was in his hand and he brought it down hard, he only managed to squash a few stragglers.

Shit. Shit. Shit. Now what do I do? Isn't there some lawn pest stuff in the garage?

Jackie scrambled to his feet and raced inside. He nearly tripped over the lawnmower because he didn't wait for the motion-sensor light to come on. *Lawn food. Bone meal. Definitely not that! Flowering plants. Grub control. Will this even work?*

He bolted out to the backyard and began pouring the granules around the area where the worms had burrowed. As soon as the bag was empty, he threw it down and ran for the hose.

"Take that, you moos," Jackie muttered as he sprayed the ground.

"What are you doing?"

"Oh, hey, Mom. There was… a bare patch. Wanted to, uh, get it taken care of before it spread."

"Who are you, and what have you done with my son?" She went back into the house, shaking her head.

Jackie gasped. The formerly golden eggshells had begun to foam and turn to slime as the water hit them. He dropped the hose and turned off the faucet before hurrying inside.

He paced back and forth across his bedroom. *How will I know if that stuff worked? How long will it take? Should I get a shovel and try digging them up? Why did Cirrina lie about the stupid eggs? She must have known what would happen.*

His phone buzzed. The motion detector had gone off. Sickly charcoal leaves brushed against his window. *Alright, Cirrina. Time for answers.*

A short time later, Jackie strode through the giants' courtyard. The horned chickens cocked their heavy heads as he passed, then resumed their scratching and pecking. The portcullis was closed, but Jackie was wiry enough to squeeze through one of the openings in the grid. After all, it was designed to keep out giants, not humans.

The doorknob was a little higher than Jackie's head. Never was he so grateful to see a lever handle. He grabbed it with both hands and pulled his feet off the ground. The bar dropped slightly as the catch released, and Jackie let go. He pushed the door open only as much as he needed to squeeze inside.

Where to now? Upstairs? Kitchen? His eye fell on the steep risers. *May as well start downstairs.*

He started down the familiar route when Loligo stepped out of an intersecting corridor.

"Well, well, well. I recognize that stench." His mouth opened. And opened. And opened. Gaping impossibly wide, his gums were ringed with jagged teeth.

Jackie backtracked.

Tentacles shot out of Loligo's cavernous maw.

Jackie tripped over his own feet and rolled across the floor. That's probably what kept him out of the grasp of the suckered arms. In a moment, he was up and pelting down the hallway.

The giant's footsteps thudded behind him.

Jackie ducked around a corner. The first two doors were locked. The third opened, and he slipped inside. He pushed the door shut as quietly as he could. Jackie turned. There was nothing in the room but stairs.

A roar from the corridor rattled the iron-banded door.

He had no choice but to go down the dimly lit staircase. The height of the risers made it challenging to move quickly, but Jackie hopped double time to get to the bottom. He ducked behind a stack of wooden crates in a corner as the door was flung open and Loligo came partway down the stairs. The giant stood there, silent for an unbearably long time.

Jackie wondered if Loligo could hear the sound of his heart pounding against his ribs. Surely that's what he was listening to. But at last, he turned and lumbered up the stairs, slamming the door behind him.

Nearly weeping with relief, Jackie let out a breath. A low moan came from an adjacent chamber. He stiffened.

A hoarse voice called out, "Hello? Is someone there? Help. Please."

Now wary of traps, Jackie did not answer. He did, however, creep to the edge of the crates, hoping to see into the next room without being seen.

A broken sob wrenched its way out of the hidden person's chest. "Please... please help me."

Jackie moved to the other side of the stack to verify that Loligo wasn't standing at the top of the stairs. The giant was gone. Keeping to the shadows, Jackie eased silently into the next room.

It was lined with prison cells. He was in a dungeon. Jackie swore under his breath.

"Hello?" the voice rasped.

Jackie slunk toward the sound.

A man with salt-and-pepper hair sprawled on a pile of rotting straw. Jackie stepped forward, and the prisoner looked up.

Jackie's heart skipped a beat. He was looking at a middle-aged version of himself. No, not himself. "Ted? Is your name Ted Bohne?"

The man rolled to a sitting position. "Who sent you? How do you know my name?"

A tear trickled down Jackie's cheek. *How is this even happening?* "Dad? It's me. Your son."

Ted crawled to the bars. "Jackie? How...?"

"We'll talk later. How do I get you out of here?"

"I never thought... Go into the next room, not toward the stairs, the other way. Try not to look around too much at the... devices. Find the cabinet at the back. Inside, there's a lap harp. If you pluck a certain string, it will unlock the door."

"Be right back." Still in stealth mode, Jackie crept into the dimly lit chamber.

A long wooden bed frame stood in the center of the room. *That's weird.* Jackie looked closer. The headboard had two holes in it aligned horizontally. A drum with a ship's wheel made up the footboard.

It wasn't a bed.

It was a rack, a machine to slowly pull people's arms and legs out of joint. Jackie shuddered and kept his head down until he got to the cabinet. Among thumb screws, pokers, and other instruments of torture, he found the harp. Jackie tucked it under his arm and scurried back to his father.

After the sixth try, the door swung open. Ted limped out and threw his arms around his son. "We have to go. There's a secret passage under the stairs. Not sure where it goes, but it has to be better than here."

Ted tried pushing several bricks in the wall. At last, stone grated on stone and a doorway was revealed. Jackie still clutched the harp as they hurried through. Ted pulled down on one of the torches and the stones slid back into place.

Flickering orange light from widely spaced torches along the walls landed the wide passage in an uncanny valley that shoved 'cozy' into 'weird' territory. Jackie started down the corridor, but Ted jerked him back. "It may be booby trapped."

He took the lead, moving carefully and stopping every few steps to investigate the walls and floor. His hard sole clunked down onto a perfectly square flagstone. A click echoed off the rock.

"Get down!" Ted grabbed Jackie and pulled him to the floor. A curved blade swung out of a hidden niche in the wall, hissing through the air.

They crawled far enough away that they were out of the arc, should it swoop by again. When Ted got to his feet, six metallic balls, wreathed in spikes, dropped from the ceiling, chains creaking in protest as the slack played out. The sudden stop caused the balls to swing from side to side across the corridor at staggered intervals.

Ted studied the pattern. "This is going to be tough."

"Maybe not. Seems they're high enough off the floor that we can crawl under them."

"You're right, boy. Let's get to it."

Jackie winced as his bony knees ground against the stone, but at last, they made it past the spiky balls. The men stood, and Jackie began dusting off his pants.

The floor shivered. Ted looked down. "Run!"

Bricks started to fall, one by one, out from under their feet. Panic drove Jackie as he sprinted down the corridor and jumped on to the tile in front of the metal door.

He twisted the handle, but it was locked.

The harp.

Jackie plucked the same note he used to unlock the prison cell. At first, nothing happened, then the door swung open. Jackie dove through the opening as he felt the stone below his feet shift.

He rolled on to his butt. "Dad—"

Ted was nowhere to be seen.

Jackie crawled to the edge and found his father dangling from the bottom of the door jamb. His feet struggled for purchase against the slick wall beneath the door, and his fingers were slipping.

"Dad!" Jackie braced one leg against the door frame and grabbed Ted's wrists. He pulled with all his strength, and just when he thought he could hold on no longer, one of his father's boots swung up onto the solid floor. Jackie tugged on Ted's belt until the older man was safely through the doorway.

The two lay on the cold floor, panting.

At last, Ted spoke. "That was close. Gotta keep moving."

Jackie kept his tongue as he struggled to his feet. This section of the passageway was free of traps, but it did dead end.

How are we going to go back? There's no floor in that other corridor.

Ted pulled on an empty torch sconce in the wall and the bricks slid apart. They peered cautiously through the doorway and found themselves looking out on the courtyard.

"Don't run." Ted rested his hand on Jackie's shoulder. "Those damn birds..."

Jackie nodded, and they walked out into the twilight-shrouded yard.

The chickens had crowded together in a corner, huddling against the building. A few watched the men cross but didn't leave their group.

Father and son hurried along the path to the grotto.

When they arrived, Jackie plopped down and leaned against the back wall. "You never know when it's going to open. Just have to wait. Maybe we'll have a chance to talk."

Ted remained on his feet, stepping to the edge of the cave and peering out from time to time. "Yeah. Yeah, sure. How is your mother?"

It stung that Ted didn't ask about Jackie, since he was sitting right there. "She's fine. It's been difficult for her. For both of us, with you being gone. Have you been in the dungeon the whole time? The entire fifteen years?"

Chunk. Chunk. Chunk. The sound of hard soles and thick heels echoed off the rocks as Ted moved to stand in front of Jackie. "Look. I'm sure it has been really tough on you. I'm sorry about that. There was nothing I could do… I don't know how you did it, but I'm so grateful you found me in that dungeon."

"You're here now. That's what matters. Come home. Get a job so Mom doesn't have to work two of them. We can be a family again."

"Jackie, your mother may have an opinion about that. But you're very important to my future. I—"

Shadows smothered the fading light. Loligo and Cirrina stood in the entry of the grotto.

Loligo grinned, showing off his wicked teeth. "The time has come."

Jackie frantically slapped the cave wall, searching for any glimmer of an opening.

Ted beamed. "You're gonna really enjoy it there. Sunshine. Beaches. Very different from here."

What? Jackie stopped hitting the rock and turned to face his father, who nonchalantly snatched the harp away from him.

Loligo quirked an eyebrow. "Did you like the Passageway of Doom?"

Ted's lips pressed into a thin line. "You could have toned it down some."

The giant shrugged. "You said you wanted it realistic to bond with the boy. Sure you can open it?"

"Yep. Once we get this interdimensional wormhole stabilized, we'll run both worlds. Ready to meet your future, Loligo?"

He turned to Cirrina. "You wait here, wife. Until I call you."

Ted played some notes on the harp and the back wall of the grotto vanished. Jackie could see his backyard. It was late morning, and a black helicopter hovered above his house. *Shit. Who else is in on this?*

Loligo stooped and entered the cave.

Ted jerked Jackie's arm, pulling him to the side. "You gotta watch those big clodhoppers. Don't want you getting crushed, now."

The giant stepped into Jackie's backyard and raised his arms in victory. His muscles began to twitch. Then random groups of fibers contracted and relaxed, forming bubbles and dips over his entire body.

Jackie's lip curled in disgust. It looked like a colony of rats was running riot under Loligo's skin.

The giant's chest heaved, and he grabbed his throat, gasping for air. "What have you done?" He dropped to his knees.

Ted stepped out into the yard, dragging Jackie with him. "Oh. I might have forgot to mention that this dimension is incompatible with your energy signature. Whoops. My bad."

The bubbles got bigger, and the motion got faster. Greenish-yellow liquid squirted into the air and splattered on the dying grass. Jackie raised his arm to shield his face. With a groaning belch, all the green goo spewed up like a geyser. But instead of raining back down, the slimy stuff turned to ash, and fluttered gently to the ground, where it vanished.

"Dad! You did it! You saved everyone from the giant!" Jackie spun around toward his father.

Ted eyed the hovering chopper for a moment. "I hate to be rushed. Sorry it has to be this way, Jackie. But it takes a sacrifice of high value to stabilize the wormhole. What's more valuable to a father than his son? Your blood will form an energy reserve, kinda like a battery, as it flows into the network of tunnels dug by those bio-engineered worms all around the beanstalk. Then I can come and go as I please. Nothing will be out of my reach." He pulled a dagger from a sheath concealed under his shirt.

"Dad! No!" Jackie shrieked.

And then he noticed that the blade was the same color as the blue-grey exotic hide boots Ted wore. The same blue-grey exotic pointy-toed boots that Mr. Smith had worn to allegedly purchase Moobelle.

Ted grunted, then swayed on his feet. The dagger fell to the grass, followed immediately by Ted. A plastic dart stuck out of his back. Jackie looked up to see a sniper sitting in the jump door of the helicopter. A section of the fence collapsed, and a swarm of people in black tactical gear, no insignia, flowed into the small yard.

"Jack Bohne?" A dark-suited male with red hair appeared at Jackie's elbow.

"Who are you? What's happening?"

"We're government agents," a blond man said as he approached Jackie. "FDA." But he offered no identification. "You seem to have planted a very dangerous invasive species here in your garden. We may need to take extreme measures to eradicate it."

Jackie watched as his father was put in a strait-jacket and strapped to a gurney. "Where are you taking him?"

The redhead smiled with one half of his mouth. "We just want to talk to him. To find out where he got those beans. He'll be fine."

"Let's step inside the house, shall we?" The blond crowded Jackie, driving him in the direction of the patio. "Pack some things for a few days. It won't be safe for you and your mother to stay here while we're working."

As Jackie threw some clothes into a suitcase, he told the blond and red-haired agents all about his ordeal. They nodded along, and Red took notes. He wasn't sure if they believed him. Hell, Jackie wasn't sure if *he* believed him.

A week later, Jackie and his mom were allowed to return to their house. The fence, which had been in need of repair, had been completely replaced. There was no sign of the strange flickering beanstalk. In fact, the entire backyard had been re-sodded with fresh St. Augustine and was greener than Jackie had ever seen it, especially in November.

He sat on the patio, drinking a soda and studying for a test.

"Jackie! Dinner!"

He gathered his books and went inside.

Jackie served himself spaghetti and broccoli and joined his mother at the table. He absently twirled long noodles on his fork, thinking about the giants' dimension and the treachery of his father, none of which he'd mentioned to her. "Mom? Do you think Dad will ever come back?" He felt more dread than hope.

She sighed. "I've told you time and again that man is not worth a hill of beans. Good riddance to him!"

He knew she was right. And yet, he wished things were different.

Outside, the full moon spilled silvery light over everything below. The night creatures were coming out for their shifts—opossums, racoons, and all the others. Crickets chirped and tree frogs called to each other for one last fling before winter blew in.

And in the gap between two slabs of sod in Jackie's backyard, a tiny bean sprout poked its head out of the dirt.

Special Recipe
By A.B. Richards

ELVIN Cochon hunkered down behind the threadbare sofa. The last thing he wanted was for the Rougarous to know he was home. Benoit Hough and two of his gang prowled the Gulf Winds trailer park this afternoon, most likely looking for trouble, or something to steal. From that, at least, Elvin was safe.

There was no point in calling the sheriff's office. Duffy Hough was crooked as they come, but because his relatives made up a sizeable portion of the sparse population of Hough County, Texas, he easily cruised to re-election every time. His nephew, Benoit, was hardly a criminal mastermind, but he didn't have to be, not in the microscopic town of Gator Wallow, nestled smack up against the Louisiana border.

Three sets of hands pounded on the decrepit trailer, and Elvin prayed the siding held.

"Sou-eee! Sou-eee! Come on out, lil piggy!" Benoit shouted as the others laughed.

At this point, Elvin knew they wouldn't stop. They had committed to getting terrible gang tattoos that looked more like derpy, mangy huskies than the werewolves they were intended to be, so they would commit to just about anything. The last time the Rougarous broke in, he didn't have the money to properly repair the door. The duct-taped latch would not hold them off long. He edged along the couch and crawled out of the living room to the narrow, dim hallway. Elvin sighed as he got to his feet. It would be dark soon, but not soon enough to help him. If he slipped out quietly, he could be at least halfway to his brother Melvin's trailer before they noticed he was gone.

He dashed off a text to let Melvin know he'd be there in a minute, then hurried to the back door. Elvin stooped to stay out of sight as he skirted the rusty car on blocks and a trash-burning barrel that cluttered the tiny yard. His brother's home was two trailers down. If he snuck through the weeds at the back, the Rougarous might not notice him. That was probably too much to hope for, but at least he'd have a head start.

Elvin had just slipped behind the next-door neighbor's trailer when he heard shouts of "Hey!" and "There he goes!" He bolted as fast as his chubby legs would carry him to Melvin's door. Even with his lead, the gang was uncomfortably close as he panted on the porch, listening to his brother turn the lock. He collapsed inside and lay on the floor as Melvin slammed the deadbolt home.

It only took fifteen minutes or so for the Rougarous to get bored with banging on the door and shouting, "Come on out, lil piggies! We wanna hear you squeal!" under the windows.

"Something's gotta be done about them." Melvin peeked out the window, watching Benoit and his minions strut away.

"Yeah. But what? Anything happens to Benoit, and the sheriff'll be out for blood."

"You're not wrong." He let the curtain drop. "Let's give 'em some time to leave, then I gotta run to the store. You may as well come with."

It was half an hour later before the growl of Benoit's glass pack mufflers shattered the sticky air, then faded into the distance.

The brothers clambered into Melvin's giant SUV. As they passed Elvin's trailer, the door stood wide open.

Elvin swore. "Stop. What have these idiots done?"

Melvin pulled in and killed the engine. Cautiously, they climbed the rickety wooden steps to the stoop. Elvin sighed and scrubbed his hands down his face. His few possessions were smashed on the floor, including the framed picture of his grandmother with him and his brothers when they were little. If she hadn't left the three of them the trailer park when she died, Elvin would be homeless.

The Rougarous had taken a knife to the dilapidated sofa, and discolored foam covered the threadbare rug like rancid popcorn. The scuffed dining table he'd rescued from the curb lay broken on vinyl tile.

Melvin cocked his head. "Do you hear water running?"

Elvin ran to the bathroom. Pieces of the toilet had been scattered across the sagging floor, the valve on the water line twisted off. Water gushed across the cracked linoleum.

"I'll go shut it off." Melvin hurried out the open back door.

Anger boiled Elvin's innards when he stepped into his bedroom. They'd slashed the air mattress that he slept on and ripped his only set of sheets. To add insult to injury, someone had taken a dump in the middle of his ruined bed.

When Elvin plodded down the steps, Melvin was tossing the wrench into the back of his SUV, and he paused to look at his brother. "That bad?"

"Worse."

"Well, you can stay with me. Come on. Let's get to Thibodeaux's before it closes. Then I'll buy you dinner."

While Melvin shopped, Elvin stared dejectedly at the ramen noodles, calculating. It was almost the end of the month, and his EBT card was empty. The $3.62 in his pocket more than covered the bag of dried beans he carried. He'd planned to buy crackers, but peanut butter was out of his budget, so now Elvin was trying to figure out how many packs of instant noodles he could get with the remaining cash.

"You 'bout ready?" Melvin came up next to him, loaded basket in hand.

Elvin grabbed a few packages, and they headed to the register.

An over-sized poster spread across the wall, so people waiting in the checkout line had no choice but to see it.

FALL FESTIVAL

POTLUCK DINNER

TRUNK-OR-TREAT

GAMES * PRIZES * QUILT CONTEST

RAFFLE FOR AN AR-15 BUSHMASTER

TO FUND BULLETPROOF VESTS

FOR HOUGH COUNTY SHERIFF DEPARTMENT

A smaller poster next to it sported a picture of the grinning sheriff in his dove-grey cowboy hat.

VOTE DUFFY HOUGH NOV 4

HE'S ROUGH, TOUGH, AND MORE THAN ENOUGH!

What a joke. As usual, he was running unopposed. The last time someone ran against him, their house burned down, and they moved away.

Elvin sighed. He'd loved Halloween as a kid. His dad would put hay bales in the back of his pickup, round up the kids out in the country, and bring them all into town to trick-or-treat. It was one big party, and afterward they horse-traded treats in the truck bed until the last child was dropped off.

Nowadays, the local church had bought into the nonsense that Halloween was 'Satan's birthday'—they must never have gotten over the Satanic Panic of the '80s—and they usurped the traditional holiday with their own 'Fall Festival.' Of course, Reverend Hayes had married into the Hough family, and was living awfully high on the hog for a small-town preacher. Elvin suspected the pastor had little room to be casting stones, but that didn't stop him.

They put their purchases in the back of Melvin's SUV and walked across the street to Buford's Beef-O-Rama for a barbecue dinner.

The place was nearly deserted, highly unusual for a Saturday night. Melvin smiled at the woman behind the cash register. "Hey, Sheri. I want the large brisket plate and a coke. And whatever Elvin wants."

"Sorry boys. Buford and them's outta town in St. Louis. His uncle had a stroke and is like to die at any minute. They won't be back 'til after the funeral. We got slaw, baked potatoes, and a little bit of chili."

Since Buford's was the only restaurant in Gator Wallow, they didn't have much choice. The brothers shared a glance, and Melvin gestured to the overhead menu. "Guess we'll have two southwest potatoes with a side of slaw each and two cokes."

He paid the check, and they slid trays down the metal railing as a pimply high school kid ladled chili onto two hulking baked spuds, then dropped two scoops of coleslaw next to each.

Once they were at their table, Elvin picked up his plastic fork and waved it at Melvin. "Something has to be done about Benoit Hough. We should call George. Grandma left him in charge of the property; maybe he can figure out what to do."

Melvin swallowed a half-chewed mouthful. "Go ahead. See if he turns up. But he doesn't want to get on the sheriff's bad side any more than anybody else around here."

Elvin flipped open his small phone and punched a few buttons. "El! What's up?"

"Where ya at, George?"

"I'm good. On the way back from Lake Charles."

"How far out? Mel and me are at Buford's. Can you meet us?"

"Yeah, I can be there in 20-30 minutes."

"See you then."

Elvin snapped the phone closed and slipped it into his pocket.

When George arrived, the brothers leaned in close and told him about Benoit's exploits earlier that afternoon.

"What about a security gate?" Melvin dragged his fork through a pool of chili residue.

George scoffed. "You kidding? Benoit's got push bars on the front of his truck—he'd just drive right through it. So would half the residents in the trailer park when they come home drunk from Rayray's. That won't do anything but cost money to fix."

Elvin and Melvin took turns spit-balling ideas, all of which George shot down as being too expensive, too impractical, or too likely to draw the unwanted attention of Sheriff Hough.

The three walked out to the parking lot. George's Lexus was already running by the time they reached the cars. He opened his door and paused. "Lemme think about it and see if I can come up with something. We'll talk again tomorrow."

It had been so long since Elvin had slept in a real bed that he snuggled in and dropped off as soon as he got still.

He dreamed that he and his brothers, along with Mary Anne Simms, were roasting marshmallows around a campfire. Benoit carried a grudge ever since Mary Anne chose to go to senior prom with Elvin instead of him. Unfortunately for Elvin, Mary Anne had the good sense to get out of Gator Wallow as soon as they graduated. She was a lawyer in Dallas these days, with a husband and four kids. But right now, in this dream, she was still the honey-blonde teen he'd been hopelessly in love with all those years ago. He was just about to lean in and kiss her when Melvin poked him in the ribs. "Elvin!"

He swatted at the offending hand and turned back to Mary Anne. But she was gone.

"Elvin! Get up!"

He sat up groggily, the smoke from the dream campfire still in his nostrils.

Melvin jerked him from the bed. "We gotta get out!"

They stumbled through the smoky trailer as flames roared behind them. They ran far enough away that the heat didn't sear their skin, and Melvin called 9-1-1. The mocking snarl of Benoit's revving truck told them all they needed to know about how the fire started. As the noise melted into the darkness, Melvin ended the call with the dispatcher. The chief of Gator Wallow's volunteer fire department was married to Duffy Hough's sister. They would take their sweet time arriving.

Melvin gaped at his car. "Back for the rest of the BBQ later!" had been spray-painted across the side of his SUV. He cracked his knuckles and called his other brother.

When the pumper truck showed up around dawn, Melvin's trailer was a smoldering heap of twisted metal. The firefighters hosed down the ashes and left.

George stood staring at the ruins with his arms crossed as a tearful Melvin poked through the debris with a stick, on the off chance that any of his belongings had survived.

After a while, George nodded his head. "I have an idea. Come on. We need to do some shopping."

Late afternoon shadows stretched across the drive as they pulled up to George's double-wide. It wasn't obvious that it was even a trailer, with the wrap-around verandah and faux chimney that rose from the roof above the electric fireplace inside. There was little George liked more than hunting wild game and throwing that meat on the grill in his expansive outdoor kitchen, then lounging in or around the hot tub with his guests. He also had a fancy, gas-powered fire pit so he could enjoy the deck on chilly winter days.

"Melvin, you know that big tub I use to scald hogs? Pull that out and put it over the fire pit. You can siphon some water out of the hot tub, so it won't take long to boil. Elvin, you help me inside."

Melvin headed to the shed behind George's house, while the other two went indoors.

George handed Elvin one of the bags from their shopping trip. "I'll take care of the lighters. You open these packages of Black Cats and get 'em ready to go. Put a stack by each of the windows."

George got busy setting up his trail cams around the outside of the house.

The exterior lights came on automatically as daylight faded. It wasn't long before the angry growl of Benoit's truck approached. A wet thud sounded against the front door, and Elvin peered out the window. A small pig lay dead on the porch, its bloody innards trailing down the steps.

The rumbling truck fell silent. George turned off all the lights.

"We still know you're in there!" Benoit shouted. "Sou-ee! Pigs in a blanket, fry 'em like bacon!"

Other voices snickered and yelled, "Pig, pig, pig!"

George had all the trail cam feeds up on his phone. "Look," he whispered. "Benoit's headed for the back. Probably thinks he can break in the glass door. The other three are coming toward the front. When I say 'go,' Elvin, start lightin' those firecrackers and tossin' 'em out the windows."

Elvin moved into position.

George snorted. "Look at that, Mel. He's trying to climb up on the roof. Idiot must think that's an actual chimney. That'll make things easier."

Footfalls thudded on the concrete steps and the first hooligan set foot on the covered porch.

"Go, Elvin!"

Elvin flicked the lighter and started tossing burning strings of firecrackers out the window. Thinking they were being shot at, the hoodlums scrambled off the porch and fled into the darkness, abandoning their leader.

George opened the back door, his brothers at his heels.

"I ain't scared a you!" Benoit screeched from the roof.

"Really? Then why don't you let go of that chimney and come down here like a man?"

Benoit stayed put.

"Have it your own way." George went inside and turned the lights on. When he returned, he had a shotgun with him. He raised it to his shoulder and fired.

"Ow!" Benoit squealed.

"What are you doing?" whispered Elvin, horrified.

"It's just rock salt. Stings, but it won't hurt him."

George pelted Benoit again, and he lost his grip on the chimney. He tried to catch himself on the gutter as he rolled off the roof, but his hand slipped off the plastic leaf cover and he tumbled into the tub of boiling water.

Melvin and Elvin followed George into the church, pulling carts loaded with coolers behind them.

"Ah, the Cochon brothers! Welcome to the Fall Festival." Reverend Hayes swept across the crowded fellowship hall toward them. "Is this for the potluck?"

"Yeah. Since Buford's outta town, I thought I'd pick up the slack. Got about a hundred pounds of barbecue."

The minister clapped his hands together. "Excellent! Folks'll be happy to have an alternative to Mrs. Turner's roasted turkey." He made a face. "The ladies in the kitchen'll help you set up."

George carved, Melvin plated, and Elvin spooned on the sauce. They were down to the final couple of pounds when Sheriff Hough showed up.

He narrowed his eyes as he scanned the brothers. "Evenin' boys. Ya'll ain't seen Benoit today, have you?"

George sliced a chunk of meat. "I'm sure he's around here somewhere. Came by the house last night, but didn't seem to like our fireworks display. You're welcome to stop by and have a look if you want."

Melvin's tongs picked up the freshly carved flesh and dropped them onto a paper plate. Elvin gave it an extra-large dollop of sauce before handing it to the Sheriff.

"I'll do that." He made his way down the line, adding more items to his plate before taking a seat at one of the long tables.

A deputy came up to the serving window. "Y'all got any more a that barbecue left? I think ya could give ole Buford a run for his money, if you had a mind to."

George shook his head, cutting up the last of the meat. "Special recipe, and some of the ingredients are hard to come by."

Even after searching the house and rooting through George's garden, Sheriff Hough found no trace of Benoit. One by one, the Rougarous either met with unfortunate accidents or moved out of town, and they never caused a problem in Gator Wallow again.

Rumor spread that Benoit was locked up in Huntsville, and, as it was entirely believable, most of the townsfolk breathed a sigh of relief. None ever had any doubt he was prison-bound.

As for the unhoused brothers, Melvin's insurance payout was enough to get a big double-wide, and they lived contentedly together, knowing Benoit Hough would never bother anyone again.

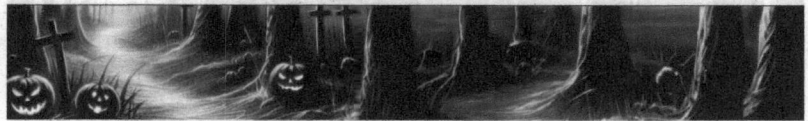

Pack of Smokes
By Holly Dey

I DON'T like October. The cold and dark season creeps in, and I want sunlight and warmth, not the cold, dreary rain that's fallen nearly every day for the past week. The sunny start this morning was a cruel tease. Only three customers the whole time I was here. People staying home don't need to buy gas. I must have dusted, restocked, and cleaned everything in the store at least twice.

Knuckles rapped against the glass. I jumped. A water-logged man in torn jeans and a denim jacket stood knocking on the door.

Why doesn't he just come in? Is this some kind of robbery or kidnapping set up? Or maybe I just listen to too many true-crime podcasts.

There are six pumps on both the north and south sides of the station, with a corresponding entrance for each.

The man knocked again. I picked up my phone and dialed 9-1, hovering my finger above the final digit as I eased toward the north door. Was anyone lurking behind him? The fisheye mirror in the corner verified no one was slinking in from the opposite side.

The stranger made the hair on the back of my neck bristle and my solar plexus tingle with cold dread. In no time, I had gone from wanting company to wanting this guy gone.

Swallowing my fear, I pushed the door open. "You don't have to knock."

The man who stepped inside looked like a drowned rat. Dark hair matted to his head, clothes soaking wet, and he was dirty, as if he'd been crawling in the ditch. Blood mixed with rainwater and sent a crimson-stained rivulet down the side of his face from a gash above his eyebrow.

"You okay, mister?"

He pointed to the bin of cigarettes above the counter but said nothing.

He may not speak English. I ran my hand along the brightly colored packs until he nodded when I touched the red one. I pulled down a pack of Marlboros and set them next to the cash register. He dug soggy bills from his pocket and dropped them on the counter, not waiting for his change. He put his head down and disappeared into the gloom and rain. Alone again, my shoulders relaxed, and my breathing slowed.

I sighed. *Better an overage on the drawer than a shortage.* My shift was almost over—Sterling should show up any time now. Saturdays were usually busy, but not today.

I grabbed a towel to wipe the damp spot where he'd dropped the money. The pack of smokes was still lying where I'd set it down. I moved the cigs under the counter, sure he'd be back for them.

The electronic buzz of the door being opened grabbed my attention. Four people scurried in. A generic sexy witch. A generic sexy devil. A man in a bad wig and wrinkled white lab coat, with a plastic tag reading "Dr. Seymour Butz, Proctologist" pinned haphazardly to his chest. The other dude wore a floral print bedsheet draped toga-style around his bare shoulders, clearly a last-minute costume improv. The rain had made his cheap foam flip-flops slippery on the tile, and he nearly skidded head-first into the Doritos end cap. Halloween partygoers dipping in for a beer run.

They almost compensated for the lack of customers with their excessive booze purchase before giggling their way out into the downpour.

They ran to their SUV, shoved the cardboard cases into the back, then scrambled into the passenger area. As they pulled out, a man sidled his Corolla up to the middle row of pumps—they had more coverage from the rain. I watched to see if he needed any assistance, but he paid outside, filled his tank, and headed east out of the parking lot.

I sighed. Sterling was fifteen minutes late. Due to the weather, I tried to cut him some slack. But it wouldn't be the first time he'd called out at the last minute and left everyone in the lurch.

Knock. Knock. Knock.

My head whipped in the direction of the north door. There he was again. *No need to make the creepy dude come inside.* I picked up the cigarettes and carried them with me at arm's length, as if they had been contaminated by the very act of him purchasing them.

Pushing open the glass just enough to reach my arm out and hand him the box, I said. "Guess you forgot these?"

He stared at me with dilated eyes and pointed up the road to the west.

What is he on?

"Can I help you with something?"

He shook his pointing hand, as if silently shouting at me. Can't define what I felt. Not fear, exactly, but some strange mix of urgency and unease.

"I'm sorry. I don't know what you want." Yanking my arm back inside, I slammed the door shut and locked it.

He bowed his head and trudged out into the wall of water.

"Sorry," I whispered as he melted into the rain. "I'm sorry." I debated about whether to call the cops to pick him up before he got run over. Better for him to come down off whatever he was on in the drunk tank than out in the deluge.

But do I really want to get involved? Perhaps I should message Tim to see if anyone's coming to replace me. Right after I go to the restroom.

I was in the back washing my hands when I heard pounding on the glass door. *What now?* I was tempted to hide out here, in case it was the wet wierdo, but I crept out to the front, anyway.

Sterling banged on the glass again. "Let me in!"

I hurried over and twisted the deadbolt open. "I thought you'd never—"

"What is wrong with you? Why is the door locked, Corrinne?"

I narrowed my eyes. "Some strange guy keeps coming and knocking on it. He bought some cigarettes, but he doesn't speak. I think he may be high or something. It's been really slow today."

Sterling shook the water off his umbrella before closing it, spattering the tile floor. "It'll probably pick up tonight. Rain's slacking off and it's the weekend before Halloween."

"Mmmm. Alright, I'm outta here."

I'd been longing for company all day, but now that Sterling was here to take over, I couldn't leave the place fast enough. I just wanted home, hot food, and my feet up… and to forget about the crazy, silent cigarette dude.

The second I clocked out, I made a mad dash for my car, where my umbrella lay on the front seat, taunting me. Didn't matter. I'd turn up the heater, and soon be home to put on dry clothes. I called the non-emergency number and told the sheriff's dispatcher about the kook with the pack of smokes. Best I could do for him.

I pulled out of the parking lot and headed west. About a quarter mile down the highway, there was a hairpin turn, with a steep drop-off into some woods on one side and a sheer rock face on the other where the road had been dynamited through the hill. I should have been thinking about driving instead of dinner, because I took the curve a little too fast and started to slide. I jerked my foot off the gas and steered with the skid.

Thought I was going to be okay until my headlights fell on the cigarette guy. He stood on the center line, pointing at the woods.

I screamed and slammed on the brakes. The car spun across the pavement, then sank into the soggy earth off the shoulder. No thud. Maybe I hadn't hit him.

My car was bogged down in the mud and hitting the gas only mired it deeper.

Great.

My hands shook as I grabbed my umbrella and cell phone. Shining my cell's flashlight up and down the road, there was no sign of him. The right front wheel hung over the edge of the drop-off. I was afraid if I got back in, it would slip over the embankment. I scrolled through my contacts until I found my regular auto shop.

Odd. I don't remember colliding with the guardrail. Darkness seeped out of the trees. Roadside assistance was taking forever.

Is that… a baby crying? I shuddered. *So many legends of evil creatures luring people into the woods by making the sound of a crying baby. Not today, Wendigo.* I stepped back onto the shoulder.

Could have been the low light, but I found no damage to my vehicle. And yet a generous section of guardrail lay half-way down the slope.

My eyes followed the trail of crushed bushes and flattened grass.

Another car! Explains the guardrail.

I hung up on roadside and called 9-1-1.

Slipping and sliding, I clambered down to the wrecked vehicle. The sound of the bawling got louder. I swore under my breath and gave the dispatcher the play-by-play.

A white sedan had crashed into a tree. Two children, a maybe six-month-old baby and a toddler, were strapped into car seats in the back. The infant was screaming, but the toddler looked asleep. I opened the rear passenger door and followed the dispatcher's instructions for checking the kids.

It hurt my heart that I couldn't hold the crying child to comfort him, but the operator said it was best to leave him in his baby bucket until EMS could check him out. I stroked his arm and talked to him as I looked around.

The windshield was smashed, and the driver's door hung open. I left the baby for a moment to look for the driver. A blue-jean-clad leg stuck out from the shrubbery to the right of the sedan. I ran over and found a man in a denim jacket lying on his belly, face turned away from me. I was not able to tell if he was alive or dead, and I was terrified to touch him. The hairs on my entire body prickled and my stomach churned as adrenaline was pumped into my bloodstream to prepare for fight or flight. He looked eerily familiar, and I couldn't bring myself to look at his face and confirm his identity.

Sirens blared in the distance. I went back to talk to the baby until the paramedics arrived.

It was then that I noticed, placed exactly in the middle of the driver's seat, a pristine pack of Marlboros.

The Favor
By A.B. Richards

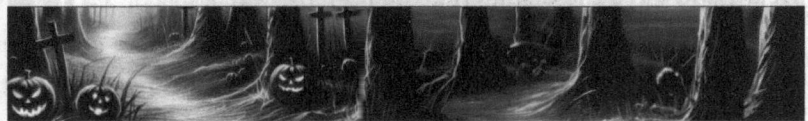

Marcus Carabas sat at his desk, imagining throwing Roger Castleton in front of the 5:15 commuter train. Not that Roger ever took the train. Maybe a sixteen-ton weight would fall on his new Mercedes instead.

He swept the plastic sandwich bag into his trash can and brushed away potato chip crumbs. The rest of the group was out celebrating David Kim's promotion with a long lunch. A promotion that should have gone to Marcus. He had been running projects—on time, at or under budget—when David was still in high school. That kid struggled to understand a Gantt chart.

But David excelled in three skills Marcus lacked—apple polishing, brown-nosing, and ass-kissing.

If Marcus had any sense, he'd tune up his resume and get the hell out of Dodge. But leaving Miller Industries would mean leaving Rachel. She was an engineer in his department. They got along like a house on fire at work. He couldn't ask her out—there was a strict corporate policy against it. And Marcus was afraid to find out whether she would actually date him if he left, and it was no longer an issue.

Sometimes it's best to let sleeping dogs lie.

He walked around the corner to the break room to wash the pickle juice off his hands. When he returned, he picked up the printout of the bid he'd been working on and slipped it into a manila envelope.

Roger had insisted on reviewing every detail, and without changing so much as a comma in the transmittal letter, handed it back at the very last minute. Marcus was never sure whether Roger was incompetent or malevolent. Either way, this package had to be overnighted today.

"Caitlyn?" *Where is that assistant admin? Haven't seen her all day.* He tried to remember if she'd gone to the luncheon. She must have.

Marcus walked the envelope down to the department admin. A row of cheerful Halloween knickknacks lined up across the edge of her desk to greet him: a black cat on a pumpkin; a cute witch in purple and green striped socks; and a family of anthropomorphic candy corn. Unfortunately, her computer was shut down and her task lamp turned off.

He poked his head into the first cubicle in the row. "Hey, Rachel? Any idea where Nina is?"

The engineer smiled. "Yeah. She had a dentist appointment. She'll be back tomorrow."

"Now what am I supposed to do with this letter? It has to be there in the morning."

"Guess you'll have to walk it down to the mailroom yourself. You know where it is?"

"Not really. No."

"Go down to the basement, hang a right. Keep going until you see the 'Miller Industries' sign."

"Ah. Of course. Thanks."

"Any time, Marcus."

"Oh, and congratulations on your promotion."

She grinned. "Thank you! I didn't get a fancy corner office like David, but I got to skip up a couple of paygrades. It's all good."

He wished he could stay and chat. But he waved and started on his mailroom trek.

The hall between the elevator banks and underground offices was lit by a flickering flucrescent light. He couldn't brush off the sense that something dark was skipping ahead each time the gloom swelled. *Of course, there will be moving shadows when the fixture isn't working right. Stop being ridiculous.* Marcus walked slower. Just in case.

At last, he found the door with a metal sign that read "Miller Industries," and opened it. The basement mail room didn't look much different from the rest of the office space. Except there were no windows to let in natural light. The bright tube lighting cast an antiseptic glare over the entire area.

"Hello?" Marcus leaned on the counter.

A wiry young man with longish black hair poked his head around the corner from the depths of the mailroom. "Oh, hey Mr. Carabasss." He drew out the s in a way that made Marcus shiver, and not in a good way. "Something I can do for you?"

"Yeah." Marcus scanned the counter and wall for a couple of seconds to find a name plate. "Tom." Marcus waved the envelope. "This proposal has to go out overnight, and Nina's already gone for the day."

"No problem." He walked across the room to take the bid package. He rubbed his collar with an index finger. "You've got a little—looks like frosting—there on your shirt."

"Thanks. That reminds me—there's cake in the breakroom on the twelfth floor."

Tom pulled a cardboard envelope from a stack and slipped the pages inside. "I'll try to remember that when I make the afternoon mail run. What's the occasion? Somebody's birthday?"

Marcus sighed. "Celebration. David Kim got promoted."

"Wow! He's so young. And didn't he just start what, six months ago?" Tom's green eyes seemed to darken a few shades as he tapped on the keyboard. "Someone like you should have gotten the job."

"Yeah, well, I guess I'll be on clean up duty. Again. I always thought if I kept the old nose to the grindstone and did good work, promotions would logically follow. I never realized I'd have to run a political campaign, too." Marcus instantly regretted saying that out loud. He was so frustrated, the sour feelings had just bubbled up and out through his mouth.

Tom carefully affixed the address label on the envelope. "Alright, Mr. Carabasss, it's ready to go." He dropped it into the tray for driver pickups, then leaned on the counter. "You know, being a mail clerk is kinda like being furniture. Nobody really notices you…." His lips turned up into a jarring smile. "You'd be surprised at what people talk about right in front of me. Perhaps I could give you some pointers on where things stand."

What's in it for him? Does he have his own payback agenda? "I see. That might b—" Marcus's phone buzzed with a text notification. It was Roger, asking for status updates on tasks that had been assigned at the morning staff meeting immediately before today's early lunch break. "Gotta run. Duty calls. Thanks for the help."

On Friday, Ravi Chaudhary, the VP of Customer Operations, called a first-thing-in-the-morning meeting. He was a recent hire and was trying to get the lay of the land.

Marcus got off the train and headed toward the office, wondering if heads would be rolling today. Most likely his, if Roger had anything to say about it.

When Marcus arrived at his desk, he found two red and gold pastry boxes, with a sticky note from Tom. "Pondicheri Fudge is Chaudhary's absolute fave."

Thanks, Tom. I'll come by and let you know how it went. Marcus managed a ghost of a smile as he set off to fetch his coffee.

Clink. Clink. Clinkity Clink.

What the heck is that? They serving martinis in the breakroom or something?

When he walked in, a young blonde he didn't recognize was pinning a notice on the bulletin board. Heavy bangle bracelets clinked together as she worked. The woman whirled around at the sound of his footsteps, sending push pins flying. "Oh! I am so sorry."

Marcus smiled. "No problem. I'll help you pick them up. I'm Marcus, by the way. Marcus Carabas. Down at that end of the building." He jerked his thumb over his shoulder. Then he put the little plastic cup into the coffee machine and pressed the button.

"Svetlana. Today is first day. New office assistant. I work with Nina."

"Oh?" Surprised by her Slavic accent, Marcus bent to pick up pins. "What happened to Caitlyn?"

"They did not tell me." She scooped pins into her open palm so quickly that some bounced out the other side.

Marcus straightened, then stepped over to hand Svetlana the tacks he'd picked up. "It's nice to meet you. Guess I'll see you around." *Hope she stays longer than the rest. She's gotta be the third or fourth one this year. Is this company so hard to work for? Or do they get paid better elsewhere? That's probably it.* He took his cup of joe and left.

Marcus began going into the office a couple of hours early and working out at the company gym before he began his work-day. He liked having the place mostly to himself when he came in as soon as they unlocked the doors. The morning exercise buffs typically started arriving as he was leaving.

On leg day, Marcus had his earbuds in and was doing ham-string curls. The workouts had started as a way to kill time, and now he was enjoying them. Whether or not he looked it, he felt leaner and stronger.

"Ahem."

Marcus yanked his head up to see Tom standing in front of the machine. "Hey. You startled me. Usually nobody else here."

"I know. Just wanted to give you a heads-up. You've been a lit-tle too helpful to David Kim. He's passing your work off as his."

"Why am I not surprised?" Marcus uncurled his lower legs.

"Well, Roger is giving a status update on current projects to the higher ups tomorrow. David's working on it, and rumor has it he's got no idea what he's doing. It might be to your advantage to have a PowerPoint prepared so you can hand Roger a lifeline and save him from drowning in bad data."

"I'd rather hand him an anvil."

"It's your job to make your boss look good, is it not? And if Ravi Chaudhary sees you being the hero…." Tom opened his hands and shrugged.

"Yeah. I guess you have a point."

"Of course I do. Welp, I have to get to work. Make good choices, Mr. Carabasss."

A shudder started at Marcus' neck and ruffled his skin all the way to his toes. *There's something wrong with that boy. He must have a beef with Roger. Anyway, the enemy of my enemy is my friend, right?*

Marcus already had most of the information he needed, and he was able to finagle the rest pretty easily. Years of tracking and managing projects had led him to develop a spreadsheet template to gather, summarize, and chart the data. All he had to do was copy the PowerPoint and re-link the tables, and he was done.

As one of the managers, Marcus sat in on the meeting. Right out of the gate, Roger struggled with the disorganized and incomplete information provided by David Kim.

"Roger?" Marcus got to his feet. "I think you must have been sent the wrong slide deck." Marcus strode over to his boss' laptop. "Let me get the correct one for you."

He closed David's PowerPoint and loaded his own. "That should fix it."

Roger's glare dissolved into relief as he clicked through the slides.

After the meeting, Ravi Chaudhary clapped Marcus on the back. "Thanks to the man of the hour! The CFO was getting a little nervous there until you jumped in to solve the problem."

The VP of Finance dropped into the conversation. "Marcus is always on the ball with the numbers. I've been trying to poach him for a while."

If he had been, Marcus hadn't heard anything about it. He wouldn't put it past Roger to secretly torpedo his advancement prospects, though.

After making quick work of his sandwich and chips at his desk, Marcus decided to go down to the mailroom to tell Tom the good news and thank him for the heads-up. As he was about to push the call button, the doors opened, and Rachel rushed out.

Has she been crying? Marcus held the elevator. "Rachel? What happened? Are you okay?"

"I'm fine." She disappeared into the ladies' room without looking at him.

What could have happened to her? After she's had a few minutes to catch her breath, she might feel more like talking about it. I'll check in on her when I get done with Tom.

When the elevator doors rolled open, Marcus hurried through the shadowy corridor to the mailroom. Tom came out of the back with a stack of overnight envelopes before Marcus made it to the counter.

Marcus grinned. "You were right! It worked like a charm."

"Of course I'm right," Tom purred. "Told you I'd help, so I'm helping."

"You should have seen the look on David Kim's face when Ravi literally patted me on the back. Roger seemed a little mad at first, but he got over it pretty quick, once he saw the slides."

Tom nodded, his head tilted slightly to one side. "About Roger...."

Marcus snapped to attention. "Oh? What've you heard?"

"Well. Actually, I'm glad you're down here, because I'm not sure what to do. I've overheard him talking about this several times, and the last time, I managed to record some of the conversation."

Tom peered over Marcus' shoulder, as if verifying that no one else was behind him. Then he pulled a silver USB drive from his pocket and plugged it into the computer. After a few clicks, the recording began to play. It was unmistakably Roger's voice.

"...need you to give me a little more time. There's a reason those schematics aren't easy to get to...yes, I have access, but if I swipe my card…you know I can't hand the money back…you will have the plans for that EBM machine next week, if not sooner." Roger's voice deepened and got louder. "Right, Nina. Five copies." There was a click of plastic on plastic. "Hey, Ravi. What do you think—" The recording ended abruptly.

Marcus blinked rapidly and shook his head. "Did I just hear Roger committing industrial espionage?"

"That's what it sounds like to me."

"Shit." Marcus scrubbed his hands down his face. "You have to take this to one of the VPs. All the VPs. I don't know. Maybe the C-suite."

"Oh, no. It *cannot* come from me. They'd be thanking me for turning him in while they were drawing up my termination papers for recording a manager."

"Well, we can't let him get away with it."

Tom rubbed his chin. "What about this? Take it to IT and tell them someone left it on your desk in a plastic bag with a note saying 'Listen' and you didn't want to plug it into your computer, because who knows where it came from? They'll find a way to play it, and you'll have witnesses."

Two days later, Marcus leaned on the mailroom counter. "I'm telling you, Tom. That was the worst thing in, I don't know. Ever. They were leading Roger out in handcuffs and during the perp walk to the elevator, he was screaming, 'It wasn't me! I did not do this!' But there was a recording. It was obviously him. I'd been lusting after his job all this time, but I didn't want to get it like this."

Tom licked his lips. "Nothing comes for free."

"That's one way to look at it, I guess."

The mail clerk's mouth twitched up into a sinister smile. "No. We had an agreement. Roger failed to hold up his end of the bargain."

Marcus took a step back. "What?"

Tom's features suddenly seemed a bit more reptilian than human. "You will do what I ask you to do, when I ask you to do it."

Marcus just gaped as the hairs on the back of his neck rose.

Tom pulled a Ziplock bag from under the counter. It contained several pieces of jewelry and Marcus recognized Svetlana's chunky bangles amongst the others. He recalled Rachel's tearful exit from the elevator and nausea squeezed his stomach. He hadn't seen Svetlana since that day. Yet another assistant admin had taken her place.

Tom continued, it what was unmistakably Marcus' voice. "Sssooner or later, the police will cop on to the fact that the one thing these girls who've gone misssing this year all have in common is that they worked at Miller Industries. In your department." He licked his lips. "What do you sssuppose they will do when an anonymousss tipsssster alerts them to check your apartment? And they find your collection of trophies?" He raised the bag of jewelry. "And of courssse, the audio journal you made about killing all those poor, poor girls."

What have I done? Bile rose in his throat, and he fled back to his office.

Quitting time had come and gone. A cold cup of coffee rested near the monitor, untouched. Its owner stared out the window into the darkness.

Marcus Carabas sat at his desk, imagining throwing himself in front of the 5:15 commuter train.

Best Served Cold

By Artemis Greenleaf

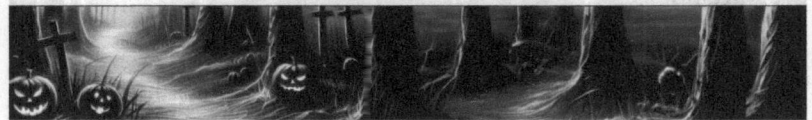

Ella pulled off her rubber gloves. Finally, the kitchen of the Any Burger was clean. Exhausted, all she wanted was rest. So much to do before Madison's Halloween party tomorrow. And Jared's on Saturday. And Valerie's movie thing on Sunday.

"You missed a spot." Mr. Johnson's nasal voice made her skin crawl. "There on the floor? Looks like somebody spilled a strawberry shake."

Didn't you make yourself one a few minutes ago? Does your mother clean up after you at home, too?

She nodded and plodded back to get the mop and bucket she'd just put away. The less interaction with him, the better. Assistant manager at a small-town burger joint was probably the highest-level job this paunchy, middle-aged man would ever have. He was surely aware of that, because he took out his frustrations on the people who were lower on the restaurant food chain than him. Mr. Johnson seemed to relish making life miserable for those who couldn't defend themselves.

Why hadn't he stayed far away in Cincinnati? Just because his great whatever grandparents lived here was no reason for him to move back. Not with that attitude, anyway. Any Burger wasn't a bad job. Until he came along.

Ella was grateful she only had to work part time. She'd have her associate's degree from Barnsdale Community College in a few months. Then it's off to the city and Any Burger would be left in her dust.

"No, Bucky! That's not right! Idiot!" Mr. Johnson snarled at one of Ella's coworkers.

A tray clattered to the floor and items skittered across the tile.

Dropping the mop, she trotted over to see the commotion. Bucky Roberts stood in the center of a debris field of orange cups, salt and pepper packets, and plastic silverware. Tears rolled down his plump cheeks.

"Don't worry, Bucky. I'll help you."

She picked up the tray, wanting to smack her boss across the head with it. Bucky had cognitive disabilities, but he was able to do most of the tasks required at Any Burger. Mr. Johnson didn't think he ought to be there, but everyone else, customers and staff alike, loved him. He was sort of like the restaurant mascot.

Ella frowned at the mess. "Go get the broom, Bucky. I'll get a trash bag."

He headed toward the utility closet.

Mr. Johnson sneered. "Trash bag! There's nothing wrong with that stuff. Put it back in the self-service area."

"But it fell on the floor."

"You just mopped it, didn't you? How dirty could it be?"

Bucky returned with the broom. Mr. Johnson loomed nearby, arms crossed.

Ella smiled at her coworker. "Can you pick up all the spoons?"

She was hoping the assistant manager would get bored with watching them and go back to his office. She'd throw the mess in the trash and restock the counter. He'd never know.

But he stood there glowering as they worked.

Someone knocked on the glass door. Bucky's father was there to take him home.

Mr. Johnson unlocked it and Mr. Roberts stepped inside.

"Hi, Dad!"

"Hey, Bucky."

Now that there was a witness, Ella smiled sweetly as she and Bucky put the soiled silverware and damp salt and pepper packets in the trash. There was nothing Mr. Johnson could do about it. They cleaned and restocked, while the slimy manager tried to make small talk with Bucky's father. Ella walked out with the Roberts men, leaving her boss to lock up alone.

Deseré Montgomery pouted at the camera, her perfect baby pink hair framing her flawless face. She waggled a tube of concealer. A ridiculously expensive tube of concealer.

She blew a kiss through plump lips. "Get this any way you can, fam! One of the best glow-up products ever, no cap!"

The influencer smeared cream underneath her light brown eyes. Ella shook her head. *Wish you had my dark circles. Then we'd see if it really works.*

Her rational mind knew you couldn't trust video. Too many filters and editing apps. But Deseré was so perfect. So beautiful. Ella wanted to be like her.

As the model spread on a layer of foundation, she spoke to the camera. "Self-care is. So. Important, y'all! If you don't believe in you, who will?"

She added more layers of makeup, then used a broccoli floret to give herself 'freckles.' "I feel we should let nature make us beautiful!" The influencer winked and blew another kiss before finishing with powder and a spritz of setting spray.

Only her signature sign-off remained. Deseré slipped into her towering, red-soled heels, picked up her designer bag—it was a different one every time—and held up two fingers in a vee. "Peace out, y'all!"

Someday. Ella sighed. She had no desire to become a model or anything similar. But she did want someone, somewhere, to notice her. To *see* her. She was invisible in this backwater town. But that would all change when she moved to the city to finish off her degree and get a job. A real job making real money. Ella couldn't wait to hand Mr. Johnson her resignation. Maybe she should put it on a cake so everyone in the store could see it.

She fell asleep imagining herself bringing in a sheet cake with the words 'I QUIT' printed neatly in red across the smooth white surface. Ella would serve each of her coworkers a piece, even the ones she didn't like. When Mr. Johnson reached for his, she'd smash it into his face.

Ella fumbled for her phone, her eyelids reluctant to peel themselves from her eyeballs. *Why is it still dark? I set my alarm for seven.*

The noise was not her alarm. It was a call from Any Burger. Tempted to let it roll to voice mail, Ella frowned at the screen. "Hello?"

"I need you to come in this morning."

"Mr. Johnson? I have class—"

"It's only for a little while. Darcy had some car trouble when she went to visit her aunt. It's fixed now, and she's on the way back, but still two hours out."

"Can't you call Tim? He's always looking for more work?"

"He has school during the day, remember?"

So do I, but that doesn't seem to bother you. "What about Heather?"

"She quit last night."

There's a shocker. "Fine. Be there as soon as I can."

Ella hit the end call button before he could reply. A couple of extra hours would be good for her bank balance. Who was she kidding? She'd be able to buy a fourth of a tube of Dereeé's miracle concealer with that money. She dragged herself out of bed and got dressed.

Where are the damn straws? Darcy should have arrived half an hour ago, and the lady with the five noisy kids under eight was pleading for Ella to hurry up. Her tiny mob scrabbled at the paper bags of pancakes and hash browns like a troop of starving raccoons.

Bucky stopped by with his trash sack and looked at her. "What you need?"

"Straws."

"I get them for you."

He set down his bag, washed his hands, and stepped into the walk-in freezer.

"Bucky? Why do you think they're in there? They don't belong…"

"Mr. Johnson put in there yesterday."

Because of course he did. "Thank you, Bucky. You're a life saver!"

"I hope I'm not lime. Butterscotch! Am I butterscotch?"

Ella chuckled. "You are definitely butterscotch."

"Better than a cabbage."

"A cabbage? Did someone say you were a cabbage?"

"My friend, Mox."

"That doesn't sound like a very nice thing to call a friend."

"Please, miss! I need those straws!" The woman with the tiny tribe shouted as the baby tugged on her earring.

Bucky scampered to the freezer and brought back two cartons.

She handed the mom a fistful of straws. Ella thought the kids would handle any extras. Perhaps it would even keep them quiet for a couple of minutes. The harried woman fled with her munchkin entourage.

"Did you know where the straws were, Anna?" Ella turned toward her other coworker.

The cashier shrugged and dismissed her with the flick of a wrist. "I'm on the register. Not my problem."

Nothing is ever your problem. Ella scowled as she checked the parking lot. *Anna and Mr. Johnson—the deplorable duo whose superpower was sucking the joy out of everything.*

Darcy's car pulled in off the street, and Ella practically ran to clock out and grab her belongings.

"Bye, Bucky! Have a great Halloween!"

"Bye!"

Ella tossed her things into her old Corolla and slid into the driver's seat. Her history class had started twenty minutes ago, and it would be over by the time she got across town and found a parking spot. She'd definitely have to go to the study group this afternoon.

Her phone dinged, and she glanced at it. Dereseé had released a new video.

"Ooooh! Halloween ideas. She must have read my mind."

She looked up to see Mr. Johnson glaring at her through the grimy glass of the Any Burger. She focused on her screen, hoping for inspiration before she and her meager budget went Halloween costume shopping.

Ella viewed Deseree's creepy doll makeup and costume tutorial twice. It looked simple enough…

Triple T Thrift, here I come.

Madison peered out from behind the apartment door's chain latch. "I'm sorry…? Wait! Oh my God. Ella? Is that you? In those heels?"

"Of course it's me!"

The door closed and metal slid against metal before it re-opened. "Come in, come in!"

Madison took the cookie tray and 2-liter bottles of cola from her and led the way to the kitchen. Next year she'd be old enough to buy alcohol, and she had the perfect Jungle Juice recipe.

An alien with enormous and disturbingly shiny black eyes stood at the punch bowl, dropping scoops of lime sherbet into the pool of lurid green liquid.

"Ella, can you help Dylan finish the punch?" Madison set the soda on the counter and whisked out of the room with the cookies.

"Guess that was her way of introducing us." Ella wasn't sure what to do with her hands. They dangled awkwardly at the ends of her arms. She tugged at her skirt, which was much shorter than she usually wore. But according to Dereseé, a mini was essential for the outfit.

Dylan nodded. "Guess so. There's some eyeballs in the freezer, if you could grab those."

"Um…"

"Don't worry. They're only lychees stuffed with berries."

Ella pulled out the big drawer at the bottom of the freezer and recoiled at the clear plastic tub of icy eyes staring at her through red, blue, or yellow irises. She knew they were fruit. Disturbing and diabolical fruit. She carried the cold container at arm's length to Dylan.

"Dump about half of 'em in. We'll need the rest for a refresh later."

"Who made these? They're creepy AF." Ella smacked the side of the container with her hand to loosen the hangers-on.

"I did. There's an Asian market two blocks from my work, so ingredients were easy."

"Ah." Ella returned the frozen fruit to its chilly storage.

In spite of knowing what was in the punch, Ella couldn't bring herself to drink any. That and the litter box cake Jared brought. Even though the decorations on top were nothing more than melted and shaped Tootsie Rolls, the thought of trying it made her gag.

Dylan was her partner in two out of the three games they played, and they won one of them. At almost midnight, Ella was picking pineapple out of the remains of the fruit salad onto her plate when Dylan came up next to her.

"You going to Jared's party tomorrow?"

"Of course! You?" The pineapple slid off her toothpick and splatted on the table.

"I was thinking since I'm staying on the same side of town as you, I could pick—"

Ella's phone rang. *Why is Bucky's dad calling me? Has something happened?*

She raised a finger, signaling Dylan to wait a moment. "Mr. Roberts?"

"Ella? You haven't seen Bucky, have you? I looked in on him before bed. He was gone!"

"Gone? How can he be gone? Where are you? I'll help you look for him."

"At the house."

"On my way."

She hung up and tossed her phone into her bag. "Gotta go. Emergency," she told Dylan, then hurried out.

Six sets of red and blue flashing lights slashed the darkness around the Roberts' home when Ella pulled up.

This must be most of the Barnsdale police force. She slammed the car door shut without bothering to lock it and rushed down the walkway. Bucky's mom must have heard the noise, because she came outside and waited.

Ella wobbled on her towering heels as she surged down the walkway. "Any news?"

Cocking her head and blinking, recognition washed over the woman's face at the sound of her voice. When Ella topped the three stairs onto the porch, Bucky's mom threw her arms around her.

"Took a minute to figure out who you were. Thank you for coming."

When Mrs. Roberts pulled away, her eyes were red and puffy from crying, and Ella felt dampness on her shoulder.

"We'll find him." She squeezed every bit of bravado she could muster into those three words.

Bucky's mother nodded and led her inside.

Doug Penobscot, the police chief, was organizing the handful of officers and volunteers into search groups. He added Ella to the search and rescue roster. He would stay at the house with Mrs. Roberts, in case Bucky came home. Or kidnappers called.

After borrowing a pair of tennies from Bucky's mom, Ella ended up riding with Cody Taylor. He'd been a couple of years ahead of her in school. She was acquainted with him, but they'd never been pals. She squeezed Mrs. Roberts' hand on the way out the door to Cody's patrol car.

More friends and neighbors were arriving as they strode down the walkway. "Chief's inside!" Ella called out. "He'll tell you where to go!" She was finally starting to feel a glimmer of hope.

Cody's cruiser was already running. He unlocked it, then shifted into reverse as she buckled her seatbelt.

"Any idea where the little guy might have run off to?"

Ella bristled. "Bucky has never done something like this before. And he may be short, but he's not a child."

"Okay, okay. Didn't mean anything by it. Our beat is the park and the wooded area behind it."

Spotlight bar scouring the green expanse, he drove slowly past the soccer field, open space, and playground. Ella shouted out the window every few yards. "Bucky? Bucky! Where are you Bucky?"

They were only a block from Any Burger. Should they try there?

Cody pulled over to the curb by the picnic area. They got out and searched under the concrete tables, behind the dumpsters, and in the restrooms, calling out the whole time.

There was no sign of him.

"We should check the woods." Cody's MagLite blazed across the dark trees.

Ella swallowed hard. Icy dread dripped down her spine and pooled in her belly. She wiped her suddenly damp palms on her tiny skirt. "Let's go."

The trail worn through the looming trunks by joggers and dog walkers was easy to follow. Ella would even say smooth. If Bucky had gone this way, surely he'd have stayed on the path instead of trying to fight through the underbrush. He may have had a disability, but he wasn't stupid.

And then she remembered where it led.

"Cody?" She had already broken into a half jog. "We need to check the pond."

"Can he swim?" The officer ejected the words on rapid breaths as they hurtled through the trees.

"Don't know."

Marie Simone she had no eyes

At the pond, none hear your cries

She pulls you in and drowns you deep

Because she wants your eyes to keep

Everyone who grew up in Barnsdale knew the rhyme. All the old stories came crashing back on Ella as she ran. She never believed them. No such thing as a haunted pond. Or Marie Simone. And yet there were generations of tales about the woman who would snatch those who wandered too close to the water. She'd drown them and steal their eyes to replace her missing ones. Encounters always happened to someone's friend's cousin. Or uncle's deceased father-in-law. The desperately unlucky friend-of-a-friend. Ella had been down there plenty of times and never once seen a whisper of a ghost.

She hadn't remembered there being a laundry-basket-sized-rock on the shore, but it might be just big enough for Bucky to hide behind. As they got closer, she was about to ask Cody to shine his light on it.

Something large splashed into the pond, tearing a hole in the mist that hovered over the unfathomable pool.

Cody whirled toward the sound. The beam of the flashlight glinted off the ripples in the murky water as the pajama-clad 'rock' shielded its eyes with an arm and stood up.

"Bucky!" Ella's feet scarcely touched the ground as she sprinted to his side. "What are you doing here?" she panted. "Everyone was so worried."

"I can go on a walk, can't I?"

Ella was taken aback by the almost-snarl in his voice.

Cody adjusted the angle of the beam so it wasn't blinding Bucky, but they could still see him clearly. "You okay, bud? We're gonna take you back home."

Bucky's lips squeezed into a scowl and his eyes flashed green in the softer edges of the bright circle of light.

The hairs on Ella's arms stood on end, and she scanned the now black glass surface of the pond. It was a bit late in the autumn for frogs, but crickets and the occasional owl were active year-round. But not here. Not tonight. Silence blanketed the brooding wood, and her own heartbeat throbbed in her ears.

The further they got from the water, the more relaxed Bucky became. By the time they had trudged to Cody's cruiser, Bucky seemed to have returned to his normal self. His warm brown eyes lit up as Ella slid in next to him in the back of the patrol car.

"Are we on an adventure?" His head was on a swivel and his mouth gaped open as he took in the sights of the night-time grounds.

Up front, Cody talked on the radio. Ella only had ears for her friend.

"I don't know, Bucky. You tell me. You're the one who led us out here."

His brows knit together. "Mox said the park would be fun at night."

Now it was Ella's turn to frown. "Mox? The friend who called you a cabbage?"

Bucky nodded.

"Did Mox come out with you? Was that who jumped in the water?"

"Don't know."

A big fish, then? "Bucky, I don't understand. Wouldn't you know if your friend came out here with you?"

The squad lurched as Cody hit the gas, perhaps a little too eager to get Bucky back to his parents.

Bucky started picking at the skin around his thumbnail. "I don't know! I don't know. I went to bed. Now we're in police car."

Could he have sleep-walked here? Can't be more than a mile, mile and a half, from his house. "Bucky, do you mind if I look at your feet?"

"Is it trick-or-treat?" His teeth glistened in the dark as he grinned.

"No, but I'm sure your mom will give you something good to eat."

Ella slipped her phone out of her bag and turned on the flashlight. He bent his knees, turning grime-caked soles up for her inspection. If someone had driven him to the park in a car, they wouldn't be anywhere near that dirty. Those filthy feet almost made her weep with relief.

"Good morning, my lovelies!" Deseree beamed at the camera. Pale, early sun streamed through the lace curtains to her left. A bookcase, filled with more decorative objects than books, loomed on her right.

Most video creators had the eerie reflections of ring lights in their eyes. Made Ella think of robots or cyborgs. Deseree did not. Ella sometimes wondered about her light source—should she research it and get one too? She dreamed of having her own channel someday.

The influencer covered her face with her hands, then yanked them away, shouting "Boo!"

The cheery room was suddenly a dark chamber, with cheese-cloth cobwebs dangling from the ceiling and bookshelf. Deseree had transformed from sunny, pink-haired beauty to a ravishing brunette in sugar skull makeup. Bright pink, orange, and green jumped out against the backdrop of her chalk-white skin. Eight hairy spider legs emerged from her blacked out right eye.

She twirled around in her outfit—a flouncy tiered skirt that fluffed when she turned, topped by a black leather and lace bustier that lifted her bosom nearly to her chin. Glittery powder sparkled on her pushed up décolleté.

"It's Halloween, y'all! Guess what, fam? I have a special guest today! Jolene Macabre is here to show you how to get this look." Dereseé pointed downward with both index fingers. "Links below. Give her a follow."

Ella rummaged through her closet. She had a black tiered skirt, though not as fancy as Dereseé's. Grabbing two tops, she moved to stand in front of the bathroom mirror. One blouse was a black satin boatneck with beaded accents. The other was a fitted purple off-the-shoulder with a sweetheart neckline that she had bought from an online sale. She hadn't dared to wear it because her sweethearts were a little too exposed for her comfort level.

The boatneck was the comfortable choice. The safe choice. But it didn't go with the skirt. Or the makeup.

She held up the purple, regarding herself in the glass. *What point does Dereseé make in all her videos? No risk, no reward. You know what? It's a Halloween party. You're not wearing it to work every day.* Ella chuckled. Mr. Johnson would probably have a stroke if she arrived dressed like that. Perhaps, on her last day, she should.

She hung up the black top. Dereseé would be proud.

Ella had planned to leave early to score a good spot. But the tamale casserole she'd promised to bring had other ideas. Dismayed to discover she had neither cornmeal nor chili powder, Ella had to make an emergency trip to the store, costing her half an hour in prep time. She left late, and, as she had feared, the closest parking was almost three blocks from Jared's house. She hoped someone would be sober enough by the end of the party to walk her to her car.

The garage door was open and costumed revelers spilled onto the driveway. Her friend always said it was better to invite the neighbors than risk having them call the cops if the music was a little too loud, too late, although he did try to be considerate. Jared's girlfriend—Mirin—dressed in steampunk attire, manned a folding table and handed out candy to shy trick-or-treaters.

The front yard had been transformed into a gothic grave-yard. Motion-activated monsters laughed, jumped, or growled at passers-by. A skeleton in a gibbet sang sea shanties.

Ella stepped into the garage, set her dish on the table with the rest, and began to search for people she knew. Most of the costumes were basic—straight from a plastic bag. A few individuals had gone above and beyond with masks or makeup, making it impossible for her to recognize them. She'd have to talk to them to figure it out.

"Ella!" Madison squealed from the drinks table. She shuffled over in her tight mermaid skirt and threw her arms around her friend.

"That seashell bra, though." Ella stepped back to admire Maddison's outfit. The clamshells were iridescent fabric appliquéd to a not-quite-flesh-colored top. A small plastic crab peeked out from her 'cleavage.'

"Girrrl. You are lookin' snatched." Madison took Ella by the shoulder and slowly spun her around.

As she faced the garage door, a werewolf with a tray of blood-spatter cupcakes made its way into the party.

Is that... Dylan?

Their eyes met across the room, and she felt an instant connection. Butterflies tickled her stomach and warmth spread over her cheeks.

Ella's phone buzzed. Fearing another mishap with Bucky, she hurried to see who was calling.

Mr. Johnson.

She let it go to voice mail.

He called again.

She let it roll again.

On the third call, she picked up, moving into the house and away from the noise of the party and Halloween animatronics.

"Ella, I need you to work."

"No."

"Bucky didn't show up, and he didn't arrange to cover his shift, so now I'm having to do it. Come in, or you're both fired."

"That isn't fair! Bucky is… not feeling well. You can't fire someone for being sick."

"But I can fire him for not covering his shift."

"I'm not on the schedule today. You can't fire me for not coming in when I'm not scheduled."

"Texas is an at-will state, remember? I can fire you any time, for any reason." He chuckled. "Or no reason at all."

Six months. Ella had six more months of school before she could see Barnsdale in her rearview mirror. There weren't a lot of part-time gigs for students in this small town, and she needed those six months' worth of paychecks. She'd grab her dad's Sunday paper and start looking for another job tomorrow. *Was it too early to scope out employment in the city?*

Yet tonight, she found no escape from the Any Burger.

Ella sighed heavily. "Fine. I'll be there as soon as I can."

By the time she located Jared to say goodbye, angry tears had ruined her makeup. Not wanting Dylan to see her in such a state of disarray, she slipped out the back door and drove home to change.

She called Bucky's father on her way to work. He told her Bucky had thrown a plate of food at his mother and bitten the dog. He never did things like that. Ever. Or walked in his sleep. They'd taken him all the way to Houston for some neurological tests.

She didn't tell his dad about Mr. Johnson's threats. He had enough to worry about.

By the time Ella arrived at the burger joint, she'd steeled herself for an unpleasant night's work. Anna leaning against the counter made it worse than she had imagined. She wanted to just turn around and return home.

Anna smirked. "Glad you could finally make it."

"Mmmm." The words Ella wanted to say were zipped tightly behind closed lips as she walked to the locker room to put away her things.

As Ella returned to the front, tying her apron on the way, she had to clap her hands against her mouth to keep from bursting into laughter.

Anna was leaning against the wall next to the drive-through, back arched and licking a soft serve cone suggestively. Mr. Johnson snapped pictures with a rhinestone encrusted phone.

Her eyes narrowed when she caught sight of Ella. "What? It's for my socials. My followers expect regular content. You know how it is. Or… maybe you don't know what popular channels are like. Are you familiar with social media?

A buzz from the drive-through menu board saved Ella from having to think up a retort to her coworker's infuriating nonsense. Anna threw her cone in the trash and pushed the mic button. "Welcome to Any Burger!"

Ella scooped frozen potatoes into the fry basket and lowered them, popping, into the hot oil while she made the Fish-A-Licious Sea Burger for the order.

It was the last customer for the evening. Everybody else must be out Halloweening. She spent the next hour wiping already-clean tables, sweeping the already-swept floor, and checking the inventory of the already-stocked self-service utensils and condiments counter. While she at least tried to work, Mr. Johnson took thirst trap pictures of Anna.

"Since the store isn't busy..." Ella cleared her throat.

Mr. Johnson's eyes were riveted on Anna's fingers, which were drawing lazy circles along her collar bone. "Yeah, yeah. Go home." Without even looking at her, he dismissed Ella with an irritated wave.

He didn't have to tell her twice. She collected her things and was in her car in no time. Jared's party was certainly still going on. But by the time she re-applied her makeup and put on her clothes, she'd be so far behind the party curve. Was there really any point in trying to recapture the moment? She could drop by as-is. Lame, but her friends wouldn't care.

Something loomed in front of Ella's car.

A woman.

Stringy black hair.

Dressed in rags.

No eyes.

Ella took all of it in as she slammed on the brakes and braced for the bump.

No bump came, and when the vehicle shuddered to a stop, she threw it in park and jumped out. There was not a soul to be seen. No damage to the steadfast Toyota. She even kneeled and checked underneath. Nothing. No creepy woman. Only darkness. *Marie Simone is a story to frighten children. She doesn't exist.*

Ella shivered and got back into her car, locking the doors behind her. She was so tired she was hallucinating. Home to bed it was.

What were the chances Dylan would be at Valerie's horror movie marathon tomorrow?

Ella had struggled to fall sleep, but once her alarm sounded, she didn't want to drag herself out from under the warm covers. She was brushing her teeth when a notification chimed. *What's Deseree got going on this morning?*

Rinse. Spit. Phone.

"Hey, hey, fam!" The influencer licked her plump lips. "Some of y'all may be feelin' a little rough today." She picked up a small plastic bottle marked 'Dr. Fillmore's Hangover Cure and Energy Elixir' and held it near her fresh, well-rested face. "The doctor here has got just what you ordered." She took a sip of dark liquid and licked her lips again.

"Now that the weather's gettin' chilly, Imma show you how to get cozy when you're chillin' at home." She blew a kiss and winked. "But you don't have to stay there." Deseree scooped a silk designer scarf from the table.

Ella watched as she folded and twisted. *Wait! I do have a scarf. Aunt Tilda brought me one from her trip to Italy two years ago.* She paused the video while she rummaged around in her closet.

Valerie opened the front door. "Look at you, Ella. When did you start wearing scarves? I love it."

"Thanks." Ella handed over a plastic grocery sack stuffed with bags of tortilla chips and jars of salsa.

She followed her hostess into the living room. Jared was sprawled in the recliner, massaging his temples. Mirin and Madison chatted on the loveseat. Dylan was not there.

Valerie dumped a bag of chips into a polished wooden bowl next to the other food. "What are we gonna watch first? Classic or new?"

"How classic is classic?" Ella spooned some fruit onto her paper plate. "*Halloween? Elm Street?* Or like black and white?"

"No black and white. No movies older than my parents."

Valerie picked up the remote and clicked on the massive flatscreen TV. The people in the commercial were nearly life-sized, and the image was so crisp and clear, Ella half expected them to step out of the frame and into the living room at any moment.

Classic won the vote. Ella set her plate on the coffee table as the opening sequence of the movie started. She snuggled against the back of the couch, sinking into the cushions. It was safe here. Easy to relax. She stifled a yawn but could do nothing about her drooping eyelids.

She watched as the scene opened on a muddy, dirt road leading into a forest. A figure loomed ahead in the trees. Ella blinked, and the figure was closer. Something followed it like a dog, except it was made of green slime, its shape constantly morphing and twisting.

She blinked again, and it took up almost the entire scene.

Filthy, ragged clothes.

Long, stringy black hair.

Empty pits for eyes.

Ella tried to scream, but the old woman grabbed her by the throat and started to squeeze with her bony fingers.

Gasping for air, Ella clawed at her throat, trying to pry off those crushing digits. Her vision went hazy around the edges and a dull red washed over the scene. She felt herself losing strength.

It was so hard to hold her arms up.

They seemed to be made of concrete.

So heavy.

Too heavy.

As suddenly as it started, the pressure released.

Ella's chest heaved, her lungs sucking in precious air. Her eyes flew open.

The scarf lay limp in her hands. The movie had been paused and everyone stared at her.

"Ella?" Valerie lowered the remote. "You okay?"

She dropped the scarf as if were a cobra, and it slithered over the arm of the couch and curled into a silken pool on the floor. "Yeah. Yeah, sorry. Bad night's sleep. I should go. I... have a lot of stuff to do, anyway."

"Ella, wait!" Jared pushed the footrest down. "You don't have to—"

The rest was lost behind the slamming door. Ella fled down the sidewalk to her car.

Thorny vines scratched Ella as she sprinted through the trees. Heavy footfalls trailed her, getting closer. Foolishly, she glanced over her shoulder and tripped over a rock. The two men were on her before she could scramble to her feet.

"What are we gonna do with her, Reverend Johnson?" growled one.

"The scriptures forbid murder. But she cannot be allowed to bear witness." The preacher stepped on the ragged hem of her homespun dress.

Ella's heart pounded so rapidly she was afraid it might explode, and her breath came in rapid puffs that made her head swim. "Please. I shall tell no one."

"Can you read? Can you write?" Reverend Johnson nudged her in the ribs with his boot.

"N-no, sir."

Twigs crunched as he stalked back and forth behind her.

"You should not have been spying, girl," the brute holding her down sneered.

"I wasn't! I was gathering wood for our fire."

"And your poverty condemns you!" the reverend thundered. "This is the church's money. I will not have it pilfered by opportunistic guttersnipes!"

Ella choked back a sob. "Sir, I had no notion of what was in the box."

Reverend Johnson jerked his chin upward, and the other man dragged Ella to her feet. From the corner of her eye, she saw the pastor snatch the spade they'd been using to bury a wooden crate. The henchman must have dropped it when he'd tackled her.

Twigs crunched and snapped behind her. She blacked out.

When Ella awoke, her head was a throbbing mass of pain. She screamed when she tried to blink, and agony ripped through her. Open or closed, her eyelids revealed only darkness. But the scream she made came out as a gurgling croak. Her tongue was also gone.

She remained still for what felt like an eternity. Weak from blood loss, she finally began to crawl across the forest floor. Ella didn't realize she was at the edge of the pond until it was too late. The clay banks were slick as glass, and she did not have the strength to stand. Even if she could, she wouldn't know where to turn.

The cold water soothed her wounds, and she had no will to move. She wasn't sure if her body was floating in the pond, or her mind was floating above her body. Everything seemed so peaceful. All she had to do was let go.

So she did.

Ella drifted out of the deep well of sleep. She sat up, scanning the room. Ballerina pink walls. A few posters. Sunlight streaming through the window. She stuck out her tongue. Still there.

Why me? Is this what happened to you, Marie? Or just a crazy dream where my mind is inventing your backstory?

The dream had cast a pall over the morning. Ella skipped breakfast. She didn't have to be to class until 11:00 so she left early and stopped by the park. She wandered back to the pond, passing the odd cyclist or dog walker on the way. Daytime transformed the woods dramatically.

As she neared the water, motion in her peripheral vision made her whip her head to the right. She caught a glimpse of Marie Simone before she vanished. Ella hurried to where the ghost had stood. A small clearing. *Is this where it happened? Or... is this where he buried the box?*

She scoffed at the idea. Surely Reverend Johnson dug it up a hundred years or more ago. Ella found a stick and stabbed it into the dirt in the center of the clearing. She'd come back later with some flowers. Now, she had to attend class.

About an hour before the dinner rush at the Any Burger, Ella listened to a textbook as she swept the floor. The front door buzzed as it opened, and she looked up to see Dylan.

"Hey." She scrambled to pull out her earbuds and pause the audio.

"Hey, yourself. Glad I finally caught you." Dylan pulled the scarf Ella had left at Valerie's house from a jacket pocket. "I've come here so many times, but you weren't working."

"Thanks." She gingerly took the silken rectangle and tucked it into her apron.

"I'm on my way back to the city. And… well, I was hoping I could get your digits?"

"You live in the city?"

"Yeah. I was visiting my aunt for the weekend."

They traded phones, and they added each other to their contacts lists.

Ella finished first. "I'm moving there the second I graduate in May."

Dylan smiled. A kind of taken-by-surprise open-mouthed smile. "Yeah?"

Ella took her own phone back as a customer pulled into the drive-through. "Gotta go. Text you later."

"You better." Dylan left the store.

As Ella drained the fries, she peered through the pick-up window. Bucky stood in the grass, staring into the restaurant. He didn't move the entire time she wrapped the burger and slid the fries into the carton. *What is he doing here? He isn't scheduled until tomorrow.* She planned to go talk to him as soon as she handed off the order when Mr. Johnston barged out the front door, muttering. "…creep…intimidate customers…run him off…"

No! He's going to scare Bucky!

She dropped a handful of ketchup packets into the bag and thrust it at the new hire at the register before racing after Mr. Johnson.

Ella nearly got hit by a car in the drive-through lane as she chased after her boss. Bucky was sprinting toward the trees, Johnson hot on his heels.

"Stop!" Ella shouted. "Stop!"

The other two ignored her, so she ran on. If Bucky was heading for the pond, this path would approach it from the west, and it was much rougher. Ella lost sight of them in the forest, but she easily followed the noise they made crashing through the brush. Once she spotted them, it seemed Bucky was skirting the water. Perhaps he was trying to make it to one of the trails?

She kept to the path they had broken through the undergrowth and was able to close the distance a little. In a clearing ahead, Bucky spun around and stopped. Mr. Johnson charged at him but tripped over a stick protruding from the ground.

OMG. Is that the one I put there earlier?

She ran past the groaning manager. The way he was gasping, she figured he'd knocked the wind out of himself when he fell.

"Bucky! Bucky are you okay?"

His eyes glittered green and his lips drew back in a snarl.

Ella nearly tripped over her own feet trying to reverse course.

"Bucky? What's gotten into you?"

"Bucky? What's gotten into you?" he aped in a nasal falsetto.

"What is wrong with you? You've been acting so weird lately that it's freaking everybody out. You're like a little brother to me. I don't want anything bad to happen to you, but you're really scaring me."

Bucky glared at her for a long moment, then collapsed. Ella ran to his side and gently rolled him onto his back. "Bucky? Bucky, are you okay?"

After several seconds that felt like minutes, his eyelids fluttered. They opened to reveal the soft brown eyes that Ella was used to. He twisted his head from side to side, taking in the canopy of trees. "Where is here?"

"We're in the woods, Bucky. Near the pond. Where you ran away to before." Ella helped him sit up. "Do you remember standing outside the Any Burger until Mr. Johnson started chasing you?"

He rubbed his eyes. "Last thing I remember is nap."

"You must be walking in your sleep again. Let's get you home."

She pulled Bucky off the ground. Ella curled her lip at the green slime smeared across the back of his shoulder. Gross. She wiped her fingers off on a clump of grass before taking his hand and turning around.

She let out an exasperated sigh. Mr. Johnson was nowhere to be seen. *Thanks for sticking around to make sure Bucky was alright. Anna's probably coming in soon and he can't wait to get to his little pet.*

Ella and Bucky picked their way through the woods until they got back to the sidewalk. They hopped into her car at the Any Burger and she drove him home. Mrs. Roberts was beside herself when they arrived. Ella thought she was going to burke him by hugging him too tightly.

"Oh my gosh!" She released her son. "I'd better call the police and tell them you've come back home."

While Mrs. Roberts whipped out her phone and began dialing, Ella smiled at Bucky. "I'm glad you're back from Houston. No more running in the woods, alright?"

He grinned at her and nodded.

Ella waved at Bucky's mother as she turned to go. Each step toward her vehicle was harder to take. Any Burger was the last place she wanted to be. But what choice did she have?

After the short drive, she parked and trudged inside. Anna was there at the register. "Well?" She slapped her palms on the counter. "Where is he?"

"I took Bucky home."

"Not him, dumbass. Reggie."

Reggie? "Do you mean... Mr. Johnson?"

"Who else would I mean?"

"Last I saw him, he was chasing Bucky into the woods."

"What?" Anna shucked off her apron and marched out the front door toward the tiny forest.

The first customer of the dinner rush pulled up to order. The new hire was walking out of the back with her things.

"Hey, wait! Can you stay a little longer? Anna just ran off and I don't think I can handle this shift by myself."

The redhead shrugged and turned around to re-deposit her purse in her locker.

Ella hurried to the register. "Welcome to Any Burger. What can I get for you?"

Watching the news on the TV in the student center, Ella gasped as Mr. Johnson's image popped up on the screen. His body had been found floating in the pond by an early morning jogger. His eyes and tongue had been torn out. Anna was there, too. She leaned against a tree, hugging herself and humming. They'd taken her to the hospital. Said she had hysterical blindness. Nothing wrong with her vision, her mind had switched off her optic nerve input. She'd be okay, eventually. Probably.

The police warned the public to stay inside after the gruesome murder—there was obviously a dangerous killer on the loose. But Ella wasn't scared of any alleged 'Barnsdale Ripper.' She was pretty sure she knew what happened.

Marie Simone waited more than a century but had finally taken her revenge. Perhaps not on Reverend Johnson, but certainly on his descendent. Unless reincarnation had come into play? Ella sighed. She had no way of knowing, but it felt like the air had cleared and this episode was over. Poor Bucky was sad his new friend Mox hadn't come by to play since they got back from the hospital. But more importantly, his episodes had stopped.

The roses in Ella's mother's garden had put on one last hurrah for the autumn. She took advantage of the empty woodland trails, clipping a few sprays of flowers and grabbing a spade.

It didn't take her long to find the stick she'd plunged into the soft earth of the clearing. She was probably just kidding herself. But what if Reverend Johnson fled to Cincinnati after he'd killed Marie without taking time to dig up the treasure? A girl could dream, couldn't she?

No student loans.

Her own apartment.

Dylan…?

Ella set the flowers aside and started digging.

About three feet down, she struck something hard. Something hollow.

The wooden box was rotted in places, but the gold coins and gemstones in leather pouches had survived all this time in the dirt.

She loaded the loot into her backpack, then filled in the hole. Ella pushed the thorny stems into the disturbed earth so it looked like tiny rosebushes were sprouting there.

"Thank you, Marie. I'm so sorry about what happened to you. I hope you can rest in peace now."

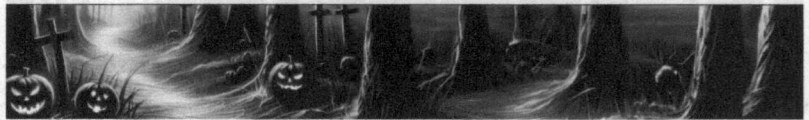

Running Shoes

By A.B. Richards

After I joined a local 'Coach to 10K' group, I lost 126 pounds. I was crazy about running.

The steady rhythm of each foot striking the ground, logging even more miles between me and my old self, made the future seem full of boundless possibilities.

My lungs pumping fresh air in and spent breath out built my endurance.

The point where the endorphins kicked in brought on the sweet euphoria of the runner's high was the cherry on top.

Running gave me freedom—as if I had been a butterfly who'd escaped my cocoon of suffocating fat. If I didn't run every day, my skin got tense and itchy.

I'd done more fun runs and half-marathons than I was able to keep track of. Finally believed I was ready for the big time. With no budget for travel, I planned to do my local marathon here in Houston. The entry fee cleaned out my meager savings account. My chances of winning were astronomically small, but I didn't care. Finishing was enough for me.

I'd really pushed myself on distance this morning and ran out of time to shower and change before meeting my mother and aunt for our Saturday lunch. Even though October in Houston can have 90° days, a cold front had brought dry, cool weather in the low seventies. We sat on the patio at Hole Mole (pronounced Holay Molay), and I'm sure the diners inside appreciated that.

Aunt Savannah arched a perfectly plucked brow as her eyes moved from my worn running shoes to my sweat-stained shirt.

"Barry?" Mom asked from behind a forced smile. "Is this really the right outfit to be wearing here?"

"I know. I'm sorry." I dipped a chip into the roasted red pepper salsa and popped it into my mouth so I didn't have to say anything else.

Aunt Savannah stirred her iced tea. "What time are you coming to Dave's house to pass out trick-or-treat candy? He told me he got something special this year."

My cousin Dave loves Halloween even more than Christmas. "Doesn't he get 'something special' every year? I was planning on a quick run after work first. It's on Wednesday, right?"

"Tuesday." My aunt set down her spoon.

"Either way. I put it on my calendar. I'm training for the marathon in January."

They congratulated me, and so did the server when he took our order. As we waited for our food, I told them far more details than they ever wanted to know about the race. Aunt Savannah's eyes glazed over, but I couldn't help myself—I was too excited. Or possibly a little obsessed—running saved my life.

The arrival of our meal brought a change of topic, and we chatted about things other than running throughout the rest of our leisurely lunch.

In the parking lot, I stumbled and nearly fell. A rush of cool air ran over my toes. When I lifted my foot to see what was going on, the sole gaped away from the upper like a slack-jawed yokel.

Great. Where am I going to get the money for new shoes this month? I got in my car and pounded my fist against the steering wheel.

By the time I got back to my apartment, I'd calmed myself down. There had to be some on sale somewhere. Even if I had to live on instant ramen until payday, I had to replace my blown-out shoe.

After about half an hour of searching, I stumbled onto an ad in the neighborhood marketplace and felt like the cat who got the cream.

A pair of Redline XLR3s. Never worn. For only $50. They were a half-size up from what I usually wore, but I had plenty of thick socks. Two-hundred-dollar shoes for only fifty? It was either a scam or the deal of a lifetime. I immediately messaged the seller.

"Shoes still available?"

"Yes."

"I'd like to see them. Is there a time we could meet?"

"How about tomorrow afternoon at 2? Japanese market on Dairy Ashford/Whittington?"

I knew the place. Also knew there was a police storefront in that strip center. Made me feel better about the seller being legit.

"Sure. See you then."

I had tried duct-taping my shoe together to take a morning run, but it only made my foot slippery in the dry grass. After I skidded and nearly landed on my butt a couple of times, I decided I was more likely to get an injury than a training session, so grudgingly, I gave up. Two o'clock could not come fast enough.

When I arrived at 1:45, I thought I'd run into the store and get a snack and a drink. I came out with a packet of mochi ice cream and a jumbo bottle of coconut water.

A lady with a bandana on her head and dusty jeans was getting out of her car with a shoe box.

I waved to get her attention as she approached. "Miriam?"

"Are you Barry?"

"Yeah."

She handed me the box. "My father died last month. I'm trying to get his house cleaned out so I can sell it. He's got a ton of stuff like this, if you're interested in more." She nodded at the shoes. "Don't think they've ever been worn."

"Oh. Sorry for your loss." I lifted the lid and peered inside. The red running shoes were pristine. I took one out and it still had the cardboard shoe form inside. I breathed deeply, taking in the scent of the leather. "These are great."

I nestled the XLR8 next to its sibling and tucked the box under my arm to get my phone from my pocket and send her the money.

A moment later, her phone dinged, letting her know it had arrived. She confirmed the transaction and smiled. "Well, that was easy. Thanks, Barry. I'll be putting more stuff up, so just let me know if you see anything else you like."

The Redlines were the most comfortable shoes I've ever worn. The brand must run small, because even though they were supposed to be a half-size too big, they fit perfectly. I was tempted to wear them everywhere, but I forced myself to save them only for running.

It was storming Wednesday when I got up for work. I went in early, hoping the weather would clear and I would be able to get a run in between work and Dave's Halloween shindig. Needless to say, I was delighted when the sun came out around 2:00.

I wish more than anything that it had kept raining.

Memorial Park was on my way home, so I stopped there. It's very popular and busy, and I usually run elsewhere. But I slipped on my red shoes and hit the trail. As I dodged around a lady with a stroller, her dog bolted after a squirrel. I got tangled in the leash and crashed into an elderly man with a cane.

"I'm so sorry! Are you okay, sir?" I held out my hand to help him up. *Totally my fault. Thought I could thread the needle between the stroller and the geezer. Should have waited.*

He rolled into a sitting position, and I fetched his cane that had been knocked several feet away.

Squatting down to be closer to eye-level, I said, "Sir? Are you alright? Do you need me to call an ambulance?"

He glared at me from beneath wiry eyebrows, then stroked a red beard that had mostly faded to grey. "Don't just sit there like a fool. Help me up."

I pulled him up and guided him to a nearby bench. He stared at my feet. "Those are some nice running shoes." Then he jabbed each one with his cane. "May they never come off when you run."

I wanted to shout at him and ask what he thought he was doing, accosting me like that, but I did just knock him down. He had the right to be cross with me, although poking me with his cane was beyond the pale. And what an odd thing to say. I cleared my throat. "If you're sure you're okay…?"

He waved me off, and I jogged away. I had been barely a quarter of a mile into my planned six-mile run. I'd have to cut it down to three if I wanted to get to Dave's on time. At least it was better than nothing.

I suppose it was the adrenaline firing extra oxygen through my body. It seemed like my shoes were carrying me effortlessly along the path. All I had to do was breathe as I fell into a steady rhythm.

Slap. Slap. Slap. Slap.

The Redlines pounded the path and settled my mind into a moving meditation. I almost didn't stop when I came back around to the parking lot. My feet just wanted to continue. I circled my car five times because I just couldn't bring myself to stop. It was like my feet had minds of their own.

As I pulled out of the lot, traffic was terrible. *Was it always like this here?* I opened my navigator app. *Fantastic.* An overturned 18-wheeler on I-10 blocked all the lanes. I crept along the congested blue path that my phone assured me was the fastest route. No way I'd make it to Dave's on time, even if I drove straight there at this rate. I wouldn't get a chance to stop by my house for a quick shower and change.

I looked down. My bored feet were marching on the floorboard. I chuckled. If people could have under-desk treadmills, I could jog in my car in traffic.

It was funny until my right foot stomped on the accelerator, and I rear-ended the Camry in front of me.

I let out a string of curse words as I pulled into the strip center parking lot behind the car I'd just rammed.

The lady got out of her car shouting, "What is wrong with you? Why? Why did you hit my car? I'm calling 9-1-1."

I opened my door and placed my foot on the pavement. Her bumper wasn't even scratched. All of my insurance info was in my phone app. But as I tried to walk over to her, my feet started jogging the other way.

"Hey! Come back here! Jerk!"

Something was seriously wrong, and I didn't know what to do. I panicked. "Help me! Help!" I yelled at the top of my lungs.

The more frightened I was, the faster my feet ran. And I could do nothing about it.

I ran for three days. Nonstop. No break to go to the bathroom, to eat, or to sleep.

At first, the hunger was like a tiger ripping at my guts, but it's mostly gone now. I got so light-headed that I often had to close my eyes and let my feet take me where they would.

I had started to hallucinate from lack of sleep. My mind felt broken somehow.

There was no part of my body that didn't hurt. Yet my feet would not stop running. I dropped my phone a while ago, so I wasn't able to call anybody and nobody had a way to locate me. I tried to flag down motorists and beseeched pedestrians for help, but they all hurried away. I probably looked terrifying by now. Perhaps they had called the police, but by the time the cops arrived, I would have been long gone.

It seemed like I would just keep running until I dropped dead, and maybe even after that. I wasn't sure if I was laughing or sobbing at any given time. I tried everything I could think of to get these damned shoes off. My feet were so swollen and painful that every step was like stomping through an infinite pit of broken glass.

Were these shoes cursed when I bought them? Or did that old man do something when he poked my feet with his cane? Hadn't he said something about never coming off?

These demonic running shoes had taken me out in the country somewhere. Hardly anyone around. Haven't seen a car for hours.

Up ahead. Is that… a trailer? Yes. Old style, long and narrow, but it had a wooden three-rail fence around it. Maybe I could grab it and rest for as long as I was able to hold on. Someone might see me outside their house and call the police, and this ordeal would finally end.

I tried throwing myself to the ground yesterday. But my feet kept running, dragging me painfully along on my back. Dried blood glued my shirt to my skin where I'd been pulled across a piece of jagged metal. I was able to get to my feet when the road the shoes wanted to cross was heavy with traffic.

As I got closer to the trailer house, no one appeared to be home—no vehicles outside and no lights inside. However, I noticed a stack of split wood.

And it gave me an idea. A horrible, terrifying idea. But it might work. With any luck, they would have left the ax out.

Tears mingled with sweat, and I wasn't sure if I wept from fear or relief. Perhaps both. And if my plan killed me, well, it was better than this. How was it that the very thing that had given me so much joy was now actively trying to murder me?

I underestimated my speed. When I shot my arm out to grab the fence post, my fingernails slammed into the wood. A couple of them bent backwards and broke in the quick. Somehow, I managed to crook my elbow around the post.

Wedging my upper body between two of the horizontal boards earned me a shoulder full of splinters. The corner post came up quickly, and I wrapped both arms around it. After a discouraging few tries, I finally kicked my right leg up behind me and hooked my heel over the middle board, then raised myself enough to keep both feet off the ground.

Confused by the lack of pavement, the shoes stopped their obsessive striding. I was already exhausted and knew I wouldn't be able to hold this position long. I evaluated my situation. If I managed to get both legs over the top, I would jump toward the pile of wood and take the chance, however small, of grabbing the ax.

As I struggled to get my legs over, I tried shucking off my shoes against the rails of the fence. They may as well have been glued to my feet. At last, I teetered on the edge of the board. The hellish shoes seemed to sense the ground and began moving my feet, but in baby steps, not loping strides.

I flung myself at the woodpile, rolling until I was against the trailer's side. Fighting the churning of my feet, I crawled on my elbows, inch by inch, until the handle of the ax was within my grasp.

With a grunt, I propelled myself forward and my fingers touched the smooth handle. I barely caught it as my feet dragged me away. I curled my body around a post near the gate. My running feet ground my hipbones into the wood, and I wondered if they would break.

Even as I wanted the homeowner or a neighbor to see the crazy-looking man in the yard with an ax and call 9-1-1, I couldn't wait for help to arrive.

I was awash in so much pain that the first chop of the ax against my ankle was barely a ripple in that great sea. I watched as blood dyed the splintered white bone to red and I struck the next blow.

When I opened my eyes, I was in a hospital room. A nurse was in the middle of hanging a new IV bag and she smiled at me. "Hello, Barry. How do you feel?"

I felt nothing. Not the stiff sheet. Not the nubby cotton blanket. Not my body lying in the bed. I could have answered her, I supposed, but what would be the point?

She waited several seconds for my reply, then gave up. "I'll let the doctor know you're awake."

My eyes followed her out of the room, but I had no strength to do more.

Two doctors came in. One told me about how the homeowner had found me lying in the yard next to a bloody ax. The person who had attacked me must have taken my shoes and feet away with them, because they were not at the scene.

I wanted to laugh. If I told them what had really happened, they would never believe me. I'd be doped up in a rubber room for the rest of my life.

Time passed and my wounds healed. I got prosthetic feet and went to physical therapy every day to learn how to walk on them. Police detectives had come several times to question me about the alleged attack, but I said nothing. I said nothing to anybody, not even my mother.

One evening in late October, I was sitting on the front porch of her house, drinking hot tea and reading an ebook. My ears caught a familiar rhythm.

Slap. Slap. Slap. Slap.

A jogger. I looked up, but no person met my gaze through the hazy twilight.

My eyes fell upon a pair of red shoes. Bone, bleached white and ragged, protruded from the top.

The accursed shoes were still running, with my feet trapped inside.

I started to scream, and I'm not sure I'll ever be able to stop.

Forgotten
By A.B. Richards

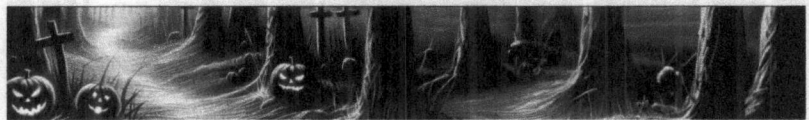

Felina Diaz sat in the common room at Myrtles Manor and stared out the window as the angry skies hurled down buckets of water and pebbles of hail. She hated the rain.

Every time it rained, someone died.

It had been 527 days since her son and his family had visited her. Not that she was counting. He'd gotten a fancy job in Jackson, Mississippi, and stuffed her in this last-resort nursing home in Slidell, across the lake from her beloved New Orleans.

She told herself that the children were very young, and it was hard to travel with a toddler and a newborn, especially after Marcia's difficult pregnancy. They would come more often when the kids were a little easier to manage. Felina just hoped she was still around then.

Max LaFont slumped into the armchair next to her. "Hey, Lina."

She turned to him with a smile. The thrice-divorced homicide detective had no family to take him in when his home had flooded out two hurricanes ago, so he wound up at the Myrtles with the other jetsam. "Hey, Max. We practicing this afternoon?"

"Guess it depends on how Jack's feeling when he gets back from his MRI."

"I'd forgotten about that."

Long years in the construction industry had taken their toll on Jack's body. But that hadn't stopped him from learning to play the trombone for their Dixieland jazz quartet. They were in no danger of getting a record deal, but they had fun. It was one of the few things that lessened the gloom of the decomposing Myrtles.

But now, they were down to a trio. Efram—the trumpet player—had lost his battle with cancer a week ago. I had rained that night, too. The owners had allowed Felina, Jack, and Max to play *When the Saints Go Marching In* in the common room as a memorial.

Felina sighed and crossed her hands in her lap. "What about the new guy?"

"What about him?"

"Do you think he plays an instrument? I mean, no one else around here is in any shape to blow a horn."

Max eyed a wiry man with huge coke-bottle glasses. "We can ask."

His knees crackled as he stood.

"Well, don't just stand there." Felina reached out her hand. Her hip replacement hadn't been as successful as it should have.

Max helped her out of the chair and the pair hobbled over to where the lanky newcomer sat reading a large-print book at one of the round tables near the bookshelves.

"Hey there." Felina pushed her top dentures back into place with her tongue before she smiled at him.

The man looked at them blankly for a few moments, then reached up to his ear to turn up his hearing aid. "Can I help you?"

Max pulled out a chair and sat down. "We just wanted to introduce ourselves and say hey."

Felina did the same. "I'm Felina. This is Max."

The new resident cast his eyes from one to the other. "Alvin. Alvin Crowley. It's nice to meet you. Thanks for stopping by." He raised a hand toward his ear.

"Wait!" Felina leaned forward, resting her elbows on the table. "We need to talk to you for a minute."

Alvin dropped his hand to his book. "What about?"

Max scootched his chair over so that he was just inside Alvin's personal space. "Lina here was saying how you looked pretty fit, for someone living at the Myrtles. We were wondering—"

Alvin recoiled and held up his hands. "No. I'm not into..." he trailed off as his eyes darted between Felina and Max.

"You don't like Dixieland?" Felina raised her eyebrows to make her lids look less droopy.

"What?"

Max chuckled. "I think you got the wrong end of the stick. Do you play any kind of music? We need a trumpet player for our jazz band."

Alvin cocked his head. "Trumpet. Player. You said 'band.' I believe you mean 'duet.' Only two of you."

Felina leaned on the table and smiled. "Jack plays trombone. He's at a doctor appointment. We had a trumpet until a week ago."

Both Felina and Max raised their heads and gazed up at the stained ceiling tiles.

Alvin followed their eyes for a moment, then sucked his teeth. "Look, I played cornet in junior high. I was consistently last chair and didn't make the cut for the high school band. Plus, it was more than sixty years ago. Don't see how I can help you."

Max grinned. "No problem. Jack had never touched any kind of instrument, and he was able to pick up the 'bone. You've got a leg up on him. It's not like you're auditioning for the Louisiana Philharmonic—just a fun little thing we do to fight off the monotony."

"The residents love it when we put on a concert," Felina chimed in. "Lila Henderson never says anything, does nothing but stare into space. But when we play, she smiles."

"Fine. I'll think about it and let you know. If you don't mind, I'm at a really meaty bit of my book."

"Great. Thanks." Max noisily got to his feet.

Felina was able to get out of the lightly padded chair on her own. "That's all we ask! Enjoy your reading."

Alvin nodded and turned his hearing aid back down.

Max and Felina returned to their armchairs.

She sighed. "Pretty sure that's a no."

He smiled. "Give him a few days for the boredom to set in."

As Felina made her way to breakfast, she noticed a couple of nurses standing in the open doorway of DeShawn Lamar's room. His wheelchair stood empty in the hall. One nurse saw her, and she nudged the other. They stepped inside and closed the door.

Not DeShawn! Why did the rain have to take him?

He'd been a bright light at the gloomy Myrtles. Always ready for 42 and played a mean game of *Settlers of Catan.* Had an encyclopedic knowledge of the City of New Orleans. Felina had lived there almost her entire 76 years, and he often surprised her with some factoid or anecdote from his seemingly inexhaustible supply. She'd miss his quick smile and infectious laugh.

Her heart was a millstone in her chest as she plodded into the dining room. Max was already at a table and Jack was getting his tray. Felina didn't feel like eating, so she visited the coffee station, then sat next to Max.

Chewing, he cheerfully waved a cream-cheese smeared bagel half at her. "Morning!" His lips pursed. "You okay?"

"It was DeShawn."

"Damn." His smile fell faster than a bank balance at Christmas,

Jack set his breakfast on the table and sighed. "Who was it?"

"DeShawn," Max answered.

Jack bowed his head. "That's a hard one."

The men picked at their food, and Felina stared into her coffee mug.

"Were storms always like this? Stealing souls away? Just so many people around us we never noticed because we didn't know them?" Jack set his butter knife down.

"Doubt it." Max pushed his reconstituted powdered eggs around on his plate.

"I don't think it's the rain." Felina's cup clunked on the table. "I think it's something that comes *with* the rain. Maybe it lives in that swamp behind the Myrtles."

Max laid his hand on hers. "Look. I'm not sure those two things are connected. Remember that most of the residents are elderly and in poor health. And you know how much it rains around here. Probably just a coincidence."

"I disagree." Felina swirled the dregs of her coffee in the bottom of her cup.

"So, test your theory." Max set down his fork. "Make a logbook. Write down the date somebody dies and the weather. It's called data. Shouldn't take too long to see if there's a pattern."

Felina dug around in the small crossbody bag she always wore and produced a tattered miniature notebook, which she handed over to Max.

"What's this?"

"Take a look."

Max frowned as he thumbed through the tiny notepad. "Huh. Hadn't realized how many people have died here in the last two years." He closed the notebook and gave it back to Felina. "And in the rain."

She patted it and searched for a pen. "It's called data. You can take the journalist out of the investigation, but you can't take the investigation out of the journalist." Felina noted DeShawn's departure date before returning the notebook and pen to her bag.

Alvin Crowley took a couple of weeks to break. Felina and Max were playing checkers in the common room when he approached them.

"Good afternoon." Alvin clutched a book to his chest.

Felina beamed at him. "Hey, Alvin."

Max gestured to one of the chairs. "You're welcome to join us."

"I don't mean to interrupt...."

"Oh, it's fine. Max here will probably be relieved to hit pause on his losing streak."

"Heeey. I'm just lulling you into a false sense of security."

Alvin pulled out the chair and perched like a nervous bird on the seat. "So, I've given the matter some thought. If you are still in need of a trumpet player, I offer my services to the band."

Max extended his hand. "Welcome to *Beignets et Café*. You don't, by chance, have a trumpet, do you?"

Alvin slumped. "I had assumed one would be provided."

"Don't you worry about that." Felina rotated a red checker between her fingers. "We'll just need to talk to Miss Emmy. She's working tomorrow, and she'll get you squared away."

Max glanced around the room before he leaned in to speak with Alvin. "Whatever you do, don't let Twyla Guidry see you talking to her. That woman is our very own southern-fried Nurse Ratched."

"I discovered that." Alvin's eyes dropped to the table.

"Oh? What happened?" Felina set down the checker.

Alvin crossed his legs and hugged his book tighter. "I'd rather not say."

Max shuddered. "Never ask that goblin for help with a catheter."

Felina glanced over both shoulders and moved her chair closer to Alvin. "Twyla's not even a CNA. She's the niece of the owners, Jerome and Roberta Garrett. They got away with hiring her because they claimed she was studying to be a certified nursing assistant. Took her three tries to get her GED. Her online CNA course is as fake as that plastic flower arrangement at the front desk."

Alvin cocked his head. "How do you know this?"

"Sorry. Reporter's code. Can't reveal my sources."

Max's eyes narrowed, and the other two turned to follow his gaze. Twyla's shift must have started, because she strolled into the common room. She was responsible for putting up decorations around the facility. Her Halloween extravaganza amounted to a few laminated paper pumpkins that had seen better days taped haphazardly to the common area walls and a cartoonish plastic black cat wearing a purple witch's hat next to the TV.

Twyla brushed by the table where Hattie Mae Wilkins and Tip Gingrich were working on a jigsaw puzzle and knocked a few pieces to the floor.

"Oops. Sorry." She wasn't sorry enough to stop and pick them up, though.

Twyla plopped down onto the sagging sofa and snatched the remote from the volunteer who was helping Hattie Mae's husband, Gerard, find the Golf Channel. "Nobody wants to see that boring shit."

She put her feet up on the coffee table and set the channel to a reality TV stream. Mr. Wilkins hugged himself and began rocking back and forth.

"Twyla! Why did you do that? We were finally getting him calmed down."

"My show's on."

"It's streaming. You can watch it later."

"Do you really want me to go to Aunt Roberta and tell her how you're upsetting the patients?"

The volunteer rolled her eyes and laughed. "And she'll do what? Cut my pay? Do you think this place is in a position to turn down free help?" She grabbed the remote back from Twyla. "Now, why don't you toddle along to Miss Roberta and tattle on me? Let's see what she says."

Twyla's lips pressed into a thin line. She got to her feet, but being far too lazy to storm off, she ambled away, leaving a wake of curse words and idle threats.

Alvin stared, wide-eyed, while Max and Felina giggled discreetly. The volunteer was trained to work with dementia patients—a skill in high demand—and she was one of the few people at the Myrtles who didn't put up with Twyla's crap.

A short time later, Mr. Wilkins' golf tournament was interrupted by a weather alert. The hurricane in the Gulf had just been upgraded to a Category 3. The weatherman predicted a 2 AM landfall, somewhere between Beaumont and Lake Charles. It wouldn't be a direct hit, but New Orleans would still be on the dirty side of the storm. Outer rain bands should start raking the area around 9:00 PM. The meteorologist's main concern was a ridge of high pressure that had been creeping down from the northwest that might stall the hurricane's northeastern trek and cause widespread flooding. He strongly recommended that people in low-lying areas evacuate to higher ground and reminded viewers that tonight's annual Halloween parade had been canceled. Stay home, stay safe.

Felina suddenly felt cold. *Who's it going to take tonight?*

Max chewed the inside of his cheek. "Maybe tonight'll be different."

"I hope so."

She absently fingered the silver and obsidian pendant she always wore. It meant the world to Felina because her late husband, Marty, had given it to her just before he died. She was worried that it would disappear if she left it in her room. Her lab-grown ruby tennis bracelet had. She and Marty used to go to that parade every year until he got sick. She missed it. She missed being able to touch him, to feel the warmth of his hand on hers.

The day passed as days at Myrtles Manor usually did. Until after supper, when the kitchen staff tried to leave.

"Hey!" shouted one from the delivery entrance.

"Why is this door locked?" asked another.

All eyes in the common room turned to the kitchen. Two ladies in hair nets shuffled out and made their way to the front entrance, only to find that it, too, was locked. The shorter of the two rattled the bar handle and banged on the glass.

One of the nurses heard the commotion and came to investigate. "Okay. I'll call the security guard. I'm sure Rafe will have a key."

"No, ma'am. He took off to stay with family in Dallas. New baby at home, he and his wife didn't wanna take no chances." The taller cook wrung her hands.

"Alright. I'll be back in a minute."

Several minutes later, the nurse returned with Twyla. Unwilling to accept the word of the other three women, she jerked the bar handle up and down a few times and shoved the door with her shoulder.

Through gritted teeth, the nurse asked, "Does your aunt keep spare keys in the office?"

Twyla disappeared around the corner faster than Felina had ever seen her move. *Guess she really wanted to watch her shows after work.*

When she came back, Twyla had her phone to her ear. "… find the keys…office door is locked…." Twyla's brow furrowed. "Are you in the car?" Her shoulders dropped and she seemed to deflate. "Oh, okay. But—… Sure, I'll tell them. Bye."

She disconnected the call and turned toward the nurse and cooks. "They went to get some supplies, like bottled water—"

"Wait, they hadn't already done that?" The nurse's eyebrows jerked up her forehead. "They've had days to prepare."

"Well, they're doing it now!" Twyla scowled. "They locked the doors to keep everyone safe. Didn't want wind from the storm to force them open."

The nurse crossed her arms. "The storm's not supposed to make landfall until two in the morning... You said they were in the car—don't you have cousins up in Shreveport?"

"Yeah, but they wouldn't leave *me* here."

Felina *almost* felt sorry for her.

Max nudged Alvin. "Let's go check the other doors."

The two got up and started down the closest corridor.

Jack gave half a smile. The doctors had adjusted the medications he took for heart failure again, and he hadn't been up for much these past few days.

I hope he has enough stamina to help with this. Felina patted his arm. "I need to get something. Meet me by Roberta's office."

She held the walker for him as he struggled to his feet. Once he was in position, she headed to her room as fast as she dared go. The item she sought—long unused—was in the bottom of her sock drawer.

Jack had almost made it to the office by the time Felina caught up to him. She stopped him at the corner and said, "Try not to let anyone past here. If anybody comes up, talk to them loud enough that I can hear."

"What are you going to do?"

Felina brandished a lock pick set. "Get Roberta's keys."

It had been some years since Felina's breaking and entering skills were in top form, but, after a few tries, she forced the lock. A green glass banker's lamp glowed dimly on the desk. Felina sat in Roberta's expensive leather executive chair and regarded the various drawers. She started with the ones she thought were the most obvious and carried on from there.

A dark shadow moved across her peripheral vision. Felina whipped her head around but saw nothing. *Are my eyes going, too?*

She opened the bottom left file drawer. Some papers that extended from an over-stuffed Pendaflex were dragged out of a folder as she pulled the handle.

Bank statements.

Oooooh. Let's sneak a peek. There was a long list of deposits from the accounts of residents, which wasn't surprising. Until she noticed some of the names. Barbette Fontesceux was a close friend, one who had passed away shortly after Felina had moved into the Myrtles. *Why was she still paying for a room more than a year after she died?* And here was James Tapper. He gave up the ghost three months ago.

What kind of scam are they running? How are they collecting Social Security from the dead? Unless they aren't reporting them.... When Efram passed, we were told there was no funeral in Slidell because his family was having his body shipped to South Carolina for burial. Was that a lie?

A scrambling in the wall made Felina jump. *Oh, goody. Rats.* She couldn't see them but sensed eyes on her. At least, that's what she hoped was observing her.

Felina pulled the file folder with the bank statement out of the drawer and left it on the desk while she searched the office for any possible key hiding spots. The longer she stayed, the more strongly she felt she was being watched. She hurried through her rummaging, then tucked the statements and lock pick set under her shirt before she fled.

"Juh get 'em?" Jack shifted on the seat of his walker.

"No. But I found something else. I think the Garretts are ripping off Social Security. The question is, what do they do with the bodies?"

She explained what she'd discovered to Jack as they made their way back to her room where she hid both the kit and folder in her dresser drawers. "I hope Max and Alvin—"

With a loud boom, the power went out.

Felina groped her way to her window. No lights as far as she could see. "Not just us. Sounded like a transformer to me."

"You're probably right. Now what?"

"I refused to allow my son to stick me with that ultra cheap old fogie flip phone. At least I have a flashlight." Felina unzipped her bag and fumbled around until she found her smartphone. "Let there be light."

The beam was bright, but not far-reaching. Still, it was enough for them to find their way back to the common area. About half of the battery-powered emergency lights above the doors had come on, painting ragged blotches of greenish light on the floors, but leaving most of the large room in shadow.

Felina put her hands on her hips. "Why hasn't that generator kicked in yet?"

"No fuel." Max's voice came from behind her left shoulder, startling her.

"How do you know that?" Jack had sat down on the seat of his walker to wait. "Did you find a way outside?"

Alvin coughed and cleared his throat. "A control panel in the mechanical room allowed us to assess the status of the machinery."

A nurse with a flashlight approached the quartet. "Okay, y'all. We're gonna help everybody get safely into bed. Don't want to risk anybody bumping into something and falling in the dark. Come with me, I'll tuck each of y'all in."

Jack's room was first. As the nurse wheeled him inside Felina asked, "What about his CPAP machine? He needs that to breathe at night."

"You just let us worry about that, Mrs. Diaz."

Felina bristled at the brush-off, but there wasn't much she could do about it.

Alvin was next, then Max. After Felina's door closed behind the retreating nurse, she got up and padded into her bathroom. She couldn't abide going to sleep without brushing her teeth. Once she had done that and applied moisturizer, she climbed back into her bed.

Felina stared at the ceiling for a long while, worrying about the storm. About Jack's CPAP (and he was far from the only resident who relied on one). About whom the rain would take during the night.

She finally started to relax and was just about to cross the threshold into oblivion when a voice whispered her name, right in her ear. Felina jerked upright. "Who's there?"

As she groped for her phone on the nightstand, the sound of rushing water flooded the surrounding dark. She struggled to unlock the screen, then tapped the flashlight. Her room was empty. Empty and dry. She swallowed hard. *Is it coming for me tonight? Or has my imagination gone into overdrive?*

A quiet, steady knocking started on her door. Felina's heart pounded and her hands shook. She tried to call out, but the words strangled in her tight throat.

"Lina? You decent?"

"Geez, Max. You scared me half to death. Come on in."

"Sorry. Couldn't sleep. Thought if anybody was up, it would be you."

"Yeah? Actually, I'm glad you're here."

She sat on her bed while he made himself comfy in her recliner. Perhaps if she was being targeted, the thing that came with the rain would choose someone else. Someone who was alone. Guilt pricked her for wishing another would die in her place, but she couldn't help it. She wanted to see her grandchildren. Felina did not tell Max about her name being called and the water sounds in the lonely blackness of her room.

It started softly, then became deafening. Rain pummeled on the roof and battered the glass. Conversation was impossible now.

Thunder shook the building as lightning tore the sky.

In the split second of blinding light, a dark shape was silhouetted by the window.

Felina gasped.

"What? What's wrong?" Max shouted from the recliner.

Words would not come, so Felina pointed at the glass. Max pushed the lever down and the footrest snapped closed with a loud, metallic thump. Free of the chair, Max shuffled to the window and peered into the darkness.

"I can't see any—"

A clawed hand that seemed to be made of a swirling black mist shot through the glass as if it didn't exist and grabbed Max by the throat. He struggled to pry open the deathly grip.

Felina scrambled out of bed, nearly falling twice. As soon as she touched the malevolent wrist, it vanished.

Max spluttered and coughed as he rubbed his throat. "What the hell...?"

"We have to get out," she spoke into his ear.

When she turned and put her weight on her bad hip, she would have crumpled to the ground if Max hadn't been there to catch her. The sharpness of the pain brought tears to her eyes, and she groaned.

"Hip?"

She nodded.

"Where's your cane?"

"By the bathroom door."

He pulled her arm over his shoulder and helped her limp across the room. Once she'd grabbed the cane, Max kept his hand on the small of her back, and the two of them struggled into the common area. He eased Felina onto the closest sofa, then sat next to her.

"What *was* that?"

"Must be the thing that comes with the rain." Felina's breathing was shallow and ragged from the pain in her hip. If it came for them again, she would not be able to get up, much less run.

On the other side of the room, the dingy glow of a set of emergency lights smeared across a floor-to-ceiling window.

Max cocked his head one way, then the other. "Is that…?"

Felina gaped as the black fog seeped through the window, gradually pooling into an indistinct bipedal shape. The thing rolled like storm clouds toward them.

"Run, Max." Felina's voice was a hoarse whisper.

"I'm not leaving you alone with… that."

"Go, dammit."

Max did not move.

The rain thing was less than ten feet away.

Okay, Marty. Hope you're ready to go, 'cuz I'm coming. And bringin' a friend. Her hand reflexively clutched the obsidian pendant.

The monster stopped as if it had hit a plexiglass wall. Then it backtracked and melted into the darkness of an unlit hallway.

"I guess we'll never really know, but it was completely out of character for Dr. Weingarten. Anyway, the brass got nervous, and ordered 72B to be euthanized."

"Clearly, that failed."

"Yeah." Levi shook his head. "They tried to dose him with enough carfentanil to kill six elephants. Problem was, he knew what they were up to."

"What happened?"

"He ate the seamen. All three of them."

Tessa's hand flew to her mouth. "How awful."

"It was. The scientists were hoping for a cadaver to dissect, but 72B didn't seem willing to provide one. He had to go—nobody on the research vessel was safe. We had to get a guy in from the CIA's Stargate project to come teach us how to keep him out of our minds. The thing that did it for me was chanting 'mashed potatoes' and imagining my head stuffed full of them."

"What?" Tessa made a little snort.

"Don't laugh—it worked. So, we got 72B offloaded onto a cargo ship—the *Mary Fitzgerald*. The plan was to take him out to the central Gulf in the deepest water, then blow up the boat. He gets turned into fish food and the wreckage is deep enough it probably won't be found."

"What happened instead?"

"We were running a skeleton crew on the cargo vessel. Brought a Zodiac so that once we were in place, we could get back to the chase ship and trigger the explosives remotely. Two of us at the helm, and a three-man demo team." Levi returned to the couch and sat next to Tessa. "A storm came up, and the seas were heavy. We were told to stand down. We'd try later when the weather passed. Suddenly, there was an explosion, and the vessel broke apart. Chunk of metal landed on my leg and pinned me to the deck. Thought that was the end, but as the hull pitched downward, it slid off. No idea how I made it to the Zodiac, or how I stayed in it. One of the demo guys was swimming toward me when 72B surfaced and… I won't say. Don't want you to have the same nightmares I do."

Tessa threw her arms around Levi. He took her hand and held it to his heart. "Couldn't tell if he didn't see me, or if he let me live to tell the tale."

"I'm so sorry." Tessa shuddered, remembering how she'd touched Tubi's enormous, Machiavellian snout. "I'm sorry you had to go through all of that. But if you hadn't, we'd never have met, and I'm so grateful to have you in my life."

Levi leaned his head against hers. "It is what it is. But now we have to figure out how to end this once and for all. If we can take out 72B, I think the rest will disappear. He's created them, holding them here somehow."

Tessa stared at the image on the fish-finder screen. She usually enjoyed riding on Levi's boat, the *Hippocamp*. But not this time. There was something underneath them. Something huge. Normally, she'd assume it was a big school of fish, but unless they'd learned to swim in the shape of a shark, this was not good. Not good at all.

"Levi? Look at this. Seems to be rising."

"Really, 72B? A megalodon? Kinda cliché."

of Twyla's clothes, and he nearly injured himself. "What the...?" He shone his light on the pile. "Aren't those Twyla's shoes?"

Felina yawned. When the nurse brought her from recovery back to her room, Max, Jack, and Alvin were waiting for her. She was happy to see them, but still sleepy from the anesthesia. The femoral stem—the part of the artificial hip that goes into the top of the thigh bone—had come unseated and displaced during Felina's struggles during the night of the rain monster.

Max patted her hand and held up a copy of the local newspaper. "You gotta see this."

The front page boasted a full color, 10 x 8 picture of Roberta and Jerome Garrett being marched out of Myrtles Manor in handcuffs. Law enforcement officers streamed out of the door, carrying bankers box after bankers box. A 60-point headline blared, "Nursing Home Fraudsters Nabbed in Social Security Scam."

"That's great, Max. But what happens to the Myrtles?"

Jack piped up. "Oh, the state's taking it over for now. At least until the trial. If the jury says the Garretts are guilty, I think the news said they'd auction the place off. If not, well, I guess they get it back."

"An old friend told me that they've found a few human bone fragments in the garden. Hopefully, there's enough DNA left that they catch some murder charges, too." Max folded the paper.

"The garden? Where they grow vegetables for the kitchen?"

Max nodded. Jack tugged at his collar, and Alvin's skin turned ashen.

The detective gestured toward Alvin. "Did you know he was a professor of folklore? He's an expert on Louisiana. Go ahead. Tell her."

"Tell me what?"

Jack grinned. "You're gonna love this,"

Alvin cleared his throat. "Based on what Max told me about the entity, I was able to trace it to a particular practitioner, a bokor—"

"That's an evil magician."

"Yes, Max. I know." Felina blinked rapidly to keep from falling asleep.

Alvin coughed. "Anyway. His name was Martin Duchamp. The Garretts paid him to summon a water elemental to help them get rid of the bodies for their Social Security scam to work. Someone with whom I am well acquainted is a powerful mambo, and she was able to put it in stasis. Couldn't release it from its binding. Said that was really weird, because Duchamp died a few years ago. At any rate, it won't be bothering the Myrtles anymore."

Martin Duchamp! No! Marty wouldn't do something like this. Felina swallowed her emotions. "I sure hope so."

She closed her eyes for several moments, then yawned. "I am so glad you gentlemen came to see me. But to tell y'all the truth, I'm drowsy from the surgery and the pain shot they gave me—I just really need to sleep."

"You got it, Lina. I'll get your necklace to you as soon as they bring you back to the Myrtles."

"Thanks, Max. I appreciate you looking after it for me."

He held the door while Alvin pushed Jack's wheelchair into the hall.

Felina wished she could leave the bed and pace. Moving always helped her think. The best she could do was drum her fingers on the mattress.

She had met Marty when she was just a cub reporter, doing a puff piece on voodoo shops in the French Quarter. He had been a practitioner, sure, but a *bokor? No, that couldn't be right.* He attended the odd ceremony and sold supplies—mostly herbs—to the locals and ridiculous trinkets to tourists. *Mama Marie's Instant Voodoo Doll* was the top seller. Various powders in lurid Day-Glo shades were nothing more sinister than colored sugar.

But the Marty she knew wouldn't go anywhere near black magic.

When he got sick, he refused to let her take him to the doctor, said it would pass. Seven days later, *he* passed. He realized the end was coming, because he sent her to his shop to retrieve the obsidian pendant.

Marty told her that he would bind his spirit to it so that he could stay there to protect her. When it was her time, they'd cross over together. Felina had always been agnostic about the ways of spirits. She wasn't sure he was really there, but it made her feel better to think he was.

Was there a flaw in the ritual he used to conjure up this water demon? Had the Garretts done something to him? Either way, this working had been the death of him. Felina believed this with all her heart.

The Garretts would be out on bail soon, if they weren't already. She'd gone from doubter to true believer in an instant and knew exactly what to do.

In the box of Marty's things that she'd stashed in the bottom of her closet was a jar with pale grey contents labeled "Zombie Powder."

The Myrtles would see one more working before it finished decomposing.

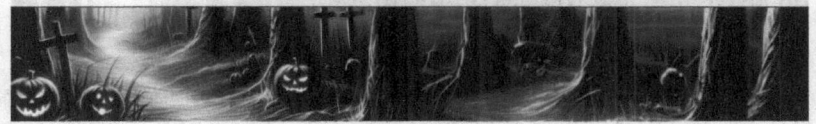

FISH TALE

By Artemis Greenleaf

"COFFEE's ready." Captain Levi Grindle dropped two slices of bread into the toaster.

"Thanks, babe." His wife set the SCUBA tank next to her pile of luggage. Dr. Tessa Whitlock kissed her husband's cheek before pouring herself a cup of joe, trying to shake off a jolt of *déjà vu*.

"Hope your dive goes well. Anything in particular you're looking for?" He sipped his coffee.

"No. Just a general wildlife survey." *As if my research mattered.*

"Let me know if you see any big fish."

Tessa chuckled. "Thought you had your own secret fishing spots."

"I do! But it never hurts to have options." The toaster popped, and he used his fingertips to nab each slice and drop it on a plate. "I had a three-day charter book online last night, so I won't be here when you get back." He walked to the table slowly—he had a slight limp from an accident when he was in the Navy. Levi didn't talk about it. Ever. But his irregular gait could make carrying liquids challenging.

"Oh." They'd had plans to go to some friends' Halloween party tomorrow. She sighed inwardly—ad hoc schedule changes being one of the hazards of owning your own business. Wouldn't be the first time she'd gone solo to a get-together. "Weather's perfect for it. Redfish?"

"Yeah. And Spanish Mackerel, if we're lucky."

Tessa downed the last of the coffee, rinsed her cup, and set it in the dishwasher. "I've gotta go. Good luck, be safe, love you." She gave him a quick kiss on the mouth.

"Love you, too."

The marine biologist grabbed her gear and struggled out the door to her SUV. It would have been easier to make two trips, but sheer bullheadedness limited her to one. It was that same obstinacy that kept her working in a field she loved, when she mostly felt she was beating her head against a brick wall.

"Diver down!" The divemaster watched Dr. Grace Gonsalves, the third of the four divers and a shark expert, splash into the water before turning toward Tessa.

She nodded and moved into position. On his signal, she stepped off the side of the boat and into the Gulf of Mexico.

She followed her three colleagues. Team leader Robin Fellowes—the coral researcher, had already melted into the murky blue depths.

Reef fish specialist Gibraltar Mayhew swam after him.

They were diving at a shipwreck on the edge of the continental shelf, and the waters beyond got very deep, very fast. They were far enough out that they might encounter orcas. While the Gulf killer whales are smaller than their brethren in the Pacific Northwest, there is a stable, yet rarely seen, population. Tessa, whose area of expertise was cetaceans—whales and dolphins—crossed her fingers.

Coralline algal nodules covered the sea floor in reds, greens, yellows, and pinks. Small, brightly colored fish darted around the structures. Tessa noted that as they neared the wreck, the nodules had faded and crumbled away. She'd expected to at least see movement, but the sandy ocean bottom appeared devoid of life. The dead zone shouldn't be this far west.

The rusting hulk of the cargo ship loomed ahead. Normally, these wrecks created artificial reefs—smaller fish hid inside from larger fish. Barnacles, anemones, and corals attached themselves to the pitted metal. But not here. *It's not like we're diving the Titanic at almost three miles down.* She checked her depth gauge—they were at 23 meters. The wreck perched perhaps ten feet from the edge of the continental shelf. Just beyond it, the seafloor sloped down sharply and blue darkened to black.

Tessa knew nothing about the history of the sunken ship—only that it was about twenty years old. As they got closer, she could make out the name painted on the side— *Mary Fitzgerald.* The boat lay in two pieces, one oriented east-west, and the other north-south, as if it had broken apart at the surface and drifted down in random positions.

Robin directed Gibraltar and Grace to the north-south section of the wreck, while he and Tessa would explore the other.

Great. While he never put his hands on her or anything so crass, he made it clear that he was interested in more than a professional relationship. Tessa was equally clear that she was in love with her husband. Also, romantic entanglements at work were always risky. Although on rare occasions, she did admit to herself that if she'd met Robin first instead of Levi, things might possibly be different.

There didn't seem to be any wildlife to survey, so it should be a short dive.

Robin paused at the gaping opening of the ship. In his search for coral polyps that needed light, he took the upper deck, leaving the deeper, gloomier lower one for Tessa.

She switched on her headlamp before going inside. The intense beam faded quickly in the liquid dark, and visibility was poor. If there was a predator lurking in here, it would see her long before she saw it. She swam cautiously, senses on high alert.

Tessa nearly screamed when an eye opened in the fragile glow of her lamp. It was clouded, as if affected by cataracts. She propelled herself backward a few feet to assess what lay in front of her and moved her head to spill light on what seemed to be a creature.

A mostly black body, taking up almost the width of the cargo vessel, was highlighted by a white underside, and an oval patch of white topped its rounded snout. Vicious conical teeth were visible in its partly open jaw. It was not an orca but looked like some ancient ancestor. An old fishing net draped over the animal, and it was unclear if it was secured to anything.

The pale eye blinked again, but the monster made no move toward her. *Perhaps it's blind and blundered into the wreckage after it got tangled in the net. Modern cetaceans use echolocation. Their early ancestors did not.* Tessa's urge to free the creature was tempered by its four-inch teeth. *If this thing is some kind of whale, it will drown here.* She'd only seen something like this in artist renderings of extinct whales. *This could be the find of a lifetime!*

She tried using her com link to request the ROV. The pilot might be able to use the robot to scrape a skin sample for DNA analysis, tag the creature with a camera, and then cut it loose from the net—all after the divers were safely back on the boat. At the very least, she needed to bring the rest of the team in to see it. The view from her body cam wouldn't be enough.

All she got on the radio was static. She'd have to swim outside the wreck and try again. *Don't worry. I'm going for help.* She started to turn around.

Wait, Tessa. The voice inside her head was breathy and old.

She froze. *Something wrong with the oxygen mix? A little shallow to get narc'd.*

I love visitors. Please stay. The white eye rolled toward her, peering out between strands of netting.

She checked her tank gauge and her regulator—there were no problems with the air.

Tessa. That is a nice name.

How? How do you know that?

Because your mind reached out to me, Dr. Whitlock. That is why we can hear each other's thoughts.

Chemicals in the water? What are you?

A strange phrase, an odd name—Sven T. Tubi—drifted into her awareness, and Tessa wasn't sure whether it had been served up by her subconscious or placed there by the creature.

There are no abnormal chemicals. I am Tubi. This is my home.

That's what you're called, as an individual. What is your species? Are there others like you?

No. I am the only one of my kind in all this wide world.

Tessa's eyes fell to the monstrous teeth. A chill rippled down her body, an image of the lifeless sea around the wreck flashing through her mind. *What do you eat?*

Tubi's mouth turned up at the corner. *What does your training tell you?*

The biologist backpedaled a few feet.

Do not worry. I find you interesting. And your research has already made an impact. You will see it is so when you return to the surface. Your dive partner is looking for you. Come for another visit soon. The great milky eye closed.

Tessa swam backward for a few yards, but Tubi did not follow. She forced her rapid breathing to slow. She was burning through oxygen at almost twice her normal rate. Robin met her a short distance from the opening, and they left the wreck together. Grace and Gibraltar were waiting in the space between the two halves of the ship. Once they were clear of the wreckage, Robin pointed up.

Relief washed over Tessa more strongly than the cool blue water. She had plenty of air to get to the surface. But she couldn't help but keep checking behind the group as they swam toward the boat. Being aware might be worse, if Tubi was powering after them.

Once they hauled out and were safely aboard, they began stripping off their gear. No way Tessa was mentioning Tubi at this point. She just about convinced herself that either the mix on her tanks was off or there was some chemical in the water. *Why else would she see an outsized killer whale telling her what she wanted to hear?*

Robin was the first to grab a drink from the cooler. He looked at Paul Cooper, the research director, and shook his head. "Not a thing down there. I couldn't find so much as a barnacle."

"Are we in the dead zone?" Tessa wrung out her hair. "I didn't think we were that far east."

"We're not. And based on the satellite, it's smaller than usual this year. Always worse in the spring and summer, when the farms up and down the Mississippi start fertilizing and pumping out the pesticides."

Gibraltar's slick, ebony skin glistened in the fading October sun as he unzipped his wetsuit. "It may not be *the* dead zone, but it's most definitely *a* dead zone."

Grace nodded. "Lotta sand down there, but not even a cownose ray. The algal nodule we swam over was teeming with fish. Then it was like someone put up a perimeter fence of death."

"How about you, Tessa? You find anything?" Paul seemed to be hoping she'd be the odd one out and have a shy shipwreck denizen to report.

"Um." *How much should I say?* "Same. Although… I do have a question. Do we have any history on the *Mary Fitzgerald*?"

Robin's brow furrowed. "Who?"

"The ship. It was called the *Mary Fitzgerald*." *Did he not see the name painted on the side?*

"Cargo vessel. That's all I know." Paul handed her a packet of roasted cashews. "I think for tomorrow, we should pull some water samples and map out the boundaries of this dead zone."

"What about sand samples?" Grace twisted off the top of an orange-juice bottle.

"Yeah. Good idea. Speaking of which… Congratulations are in order for Dr. Whitlock." Paul beamed at Tessa.

"What?" Tessa paused, a handful of nuts inches from her mouth.

"You remember that grant you wrote last month? Not only did NOAA fund it, but LUSCA Shipping is matching the funding. Seems they have some new activist board members who want to boost their green cred by reducing whale collisions."

Tessa plunked onto a bench. "Oh, wow. That's amazing… I don't know what to say. When do we start?" *Is this what Tubi meant?*

Paul chuckled. "We have to finish this project up, first. Remember to upload your camera feeds when we get dockside."

Of course! How had I forgotten about the camera? The video would show whether there really was a proto-orca. If she imagined the whole thing, she'd be glad she kept her mouth shut.

Tessa went below decks to the restroom. She watched the film, away from her teammates. Swimming to the wreck looked like any other trek through the coral. When she entered the downed ship, the image began to crackle around the edges, and by the time she was all the way to where Tubi rested, nothing but static flickered across the screen. When she left the wreckage, the video returned to normal.

Tessa lay on her bed in the hotel room, searching the internet on her phone for details about extinct whales. The closest thing she found to Tubi was a brygmophyseter, a twenty plus foot-long raptorial sperm whale from the Miocene. It didn't look exactly like Tubi, but then again, these images were all artists' best guesses, not photographs. She noted the brygmophyseter highlights in her journal at the bottom of the entry on today's dive.

She was about to get up and brush her teeth when her phone chimed. It was an incoming video chat from Levi. His image on the screen made her smile.

"Hey, babe. How's the diving?" He was on the deck of his boat, night sea breeze playing with his hair.

"Strange." She sat up.

"How so?"

"The whole area was barren. Not a sign of life. But we weren't in the Gulf dead zone. Grace said it was like someone put up an invisible fence of death around it. We're taking samples tomorrow."

Something splashed in the water behind Levi. "Hey, it's dolphins! They must have known I was on the call with you and came to say hi."

Levi always knew how to make her smile. "Wave at them for me."

He did. "So, where were you diving? Like an oil platform? Usually tons of fish around those."

"Shipwreck. East of the Flower Garden Banks, west of the dead zone. Or so we thought."

"Find any doubloons?"

"I wish. Nowhere near that old. How was the fishing? Get any reds?"

"Pulled in a few good-size bulls. Clients are happy."

"Cool. We're back at the *Mary Fitzgerald* tomorrow morning. Probably be home a little earlier than planned."

"What did you say?"

"We're taking samples. At the wreck."

"Are you sure that's a great idea?" Worry lines pinched his forehead, and the background began moving faster, as if he were pacing the deck. "If there's something in the water that killed off everything in the area, maybe you shouldn't swim in it. I think it's dangerous."

"We've been on shore for hours, and everybody seems fine. But we are wearing drysuits tomorrow as a precaution."

"I wish you'd stay on the boat."

"You know I can't do that." Tessa already had it in mind that she'd try to sneak off to visit Tubi again while the team was down there. *Surely, they'd want samples from* inside *the wreck. Could be a chemical leak from the shipwreck, after all. That might explain Tubi. Still, there was the thing about my research. Prediction or the granting of a wish?*

"Just be extra careful. I love you. Something came up, and I've gotta go. I'll call you tomorrow."

"Night. Love you."

Tessa got up to brush her teeth. As she looked at herself in the bathroom mirror, she wondered why Levi's whole demeanor changed when she'd mentioned the shipwreck. That and his abrupt disconnect made her uneasy.

Thunder rattled the windowpanes of the budget motel.

Or it could be the weather coming in...

The water was a little choppy from the storms that passed through last night, but the seas were certainly not heavy enough to cancel the dive. The four divers would be carrying mesh bags with containers for samples.

Tessa preferred diving in a wetsuit. It was thinner and more maneuverable, and even the thinnest one worked anywhere in the Gulf of Mexico. The drysuit was bulkier and heavier, and had to be worn over one or more layers of clothing. It fit loosely to allow her body heat to warm the air inside the suit. But warm air rises and tends to accumulate at whatever part of the suit is facing the surface. She'd once gotten stuck upside down and had to make her entire ascent that way.

Great. Now her zipper was jammed. "Anybody got zip lube handy?"

Robin brought over a lipstick-sized tube and rubbed it across the zipper above and below where it was stuck, from the top of her hip to just below where the diagonal zipper crossed between her breasts.

"How's that?" he asked, standing too close. His breath smelled like cinnamon.

Tessa pulled the tab down and back up a few times. "Thanks."

Before they hit the water, Paul laid out what areas needed to be tested, and how many samples to take from each one. Tessa volunteered to gather all the ones from inside the wreck while the others were exploring the perimeter.

Tessa's stomach flip-flopped the entire way down. *What if Tubi isn't there? Would that mean I imagined him? Or... that he was hunting for food?* She swallowed hard. *No, if there's a chemical in the water that caused me to hallucinate, the drysuit will prevent that. If I don't see him, it was because he was never there.*

The divers spread out to their assigned locations. Tessa hurried through the section of the ship that Gibralter and Grace had explored the day before. With her samples collected, she turned toward Tubi's hold. She pressed the button on her chest to add a little air to her suit.

Tubi?

There was no reply inside her head. Tessa wasn't sure which she dreaded more: seeing him, or not.

She switched on her headlamp. Swimming much closer to the bulkhead today than yesterday, she noticed some metal bars, perhaps a gate, twisted against the dented wall. A corroded steel placard hung haphazardly from it, moving back and forth with the current. Most of the paint had gone, but it appeared to have writing on it.

The blocky stenciled letters were difficult to make out, but she thought it said 'MALF-72B.'

72B. Seven. T. 2. B. Sven T. Tubi.

Tessa swore. He was real. But *what* was he? *What the hell is a MALF?* She studied the lettering again. *Could it be 'MALE?' No. Pretty sure it's an 'F.'*

She considered getting out of there. Without the samples. Just swimming away. Quickly.

Tessa? You have come back to see me! It gets lonely down here, in the dark.

Tubi? Yes. I'm here.

Good. Good. What are you working on today?

Taking some samples.

There are no strange chemicals in the water.

Tessa stared into the gently billowing gloom before her. Her pulse throbbed against the tight, waterproof cuffs on her wrists. *Stop burning air, you fool.*

I told you. I like you. You are my friend.

As Tessa watched, light began to emerge out of the darkness. She glanced up to see if there was a hole above where the sun could shine through.

It was not light. The white spot on Tubi's massive head moved into the puny beam of her headlamp.

He could swallow me whole without even having to chew.

I could. But I will not.

Tessa hoped he told the truth. Her body did not believe him. When she tried to swim backward, her muscles were stiff and unresponsive. Her breaths came too shallow, too fast. If she couldn't stop hyperventilating, she might pass out.

Tubi stopped less than a yard from Tessa, his mouthful of ivory daggers gleaming in the thin light of the headlamp.

Every survival instinct in her lizard brain screamed at her to flee. *Get away now!* But she was frozen in terror. Panic drowned her rational thoughts, and still she could not move.

A strangled whimper escaped her throat.

Sound entered her mind. It had a rhythm. A melody. *Is Tubi singing?* It continued for what seemed like hours. There were no words, at least not any she could understand. But she felt she was floating in a sea of stars. Planets drifted by. Galaxies rotated around them. Looming to their right, an incomprehensibly large red nebula fringed in white, was an angry, titanic eye staring into infinity.

The melody was so hypnotic, she completely forgot that an apex predator was only an arm's length away.

In her song-induced imaginings, a distant planet gradually swelled into existence. A blue marble floating in space. It got bigger, bigger, bigger, and then she was dropping through the atmosphere. With a splash, she plunged into the ocean. A school of herring circled into a sphere as she hit the water. An immense leatherback flapped by, a remora clinging to the underside of its shell. Curious dolphins came to check out the new visitor, diving and barrel-rolling around Tessa.

This. This is why I became a marine biologist in the first place.

Her skin tingled pleasantly with awe and excitement.

She continued toward the sea floor. Something dark floated below her, and joy bled into fear.

As she got closer, she realized the thing was not dangerous. At least, not to her. It was the carcass of a humpback whale, tangled in abandoned fishing nets and drowned. A shark that had come for a meal had also been ensnared. The more it struggled, the worse its situation became.

And Tessa could do nothing to help it.

Her feet landed in soft sand. She shuffled along the sea floor, scanning the rocks for life. A small octopus darted past, and she followed it. Sensing danger, it changed course and scuttled into its home—a clear plastic cup. As she searched for a safer alternative for the creature, she found nothing but trash. The seafloor was littered with garbage.

Tessa sat and wept. *I just wish this would stop. Why? Why are we so dumb? I wish the sea was thriving and not dying.*

The song stopped and instantly Tessa was back in the shipwreck. Tubi regarded her with one cloudy eye. *Then you must take your samples and go. Quickly. And yet, I feel we will surely meet again.*

Arm quivering from the fight-or-flight response surging through her body, Tessa very slowly, very carefully, gave Tubi two gentle pats on his great snout. *Thank you for the song. But your words… sound ominous.*

Go, my friend.

Tessa turned and swam toward the opening, pausing to gather a few samples on the way. She hadn't realized she'd been crying, and the hot tears steamed up her mask, so she had to clear that as well. The closer she got to the light, the more dread weighed her down, holding her inside the wreck.

When she finally dragged herself out of the ship, the other three divers were waiting for her. She patted her sample bag. Robin pointed upward. They began their ascent, with Grace and Gibraltar in the lead, Robin in the middle, and Tessa slightly behind.

Something large and dark rocketed out of the abyss. Its jaws opened and Robin was gone.

No. No. Nonono. Stunned, Tessa floated in place while Gibraltar and Grace carried on, oblivious to what had just happened. Tubi's words echoed in her head. *Take your samples and go. Quickly.*

Tessa struggled to make her frozen limbs work. Her feet churning through the water, she tapped her com link. "Mayday! Mayday! Mayday! Large predator!"

"Copy that." The divemaster's voice was reassuring. "Keep an eye on it and stay calm, but move away. Sharks are mostly just curious about divers."

Grace and Gibraltar paused and turned toward Tessa. Their heads rotated back and forth, and she knew they were searching for Robin.

Swimming wasn't fast enough. Tessa pressed the inflator on her suit. As it filled with air, she rose faster. "Not shark! Got Robin!" Tessa's head swam and sweat beaded on her forehead.

She looked down. Always a bad plan. If the thing was coming back, knowing it was behind her, destroying the distance between them....

With her position shift, her suit became top heavy, and she rotated vertically in the water. Tessa was still rising, but feet first. She couldn't spare the time to right herself, just had to keep going. With that monster nearby, every second counted.

Below, a dark mass glided over the edge of the shelf. It undulated lazily, silhouetted against the white sand. From her perspective, it almost looked like a crocodile. A crocodile bigger than a city bus. But instead of stubby legs, it had wide paddles.

That could not be. Marine reptiles that size died out millions of years ago. The com link crackled in her ear, but she could not make out the words over her short, rapid breathing.

The monster stopped. Its gruesome head twisted, and a large black eye looked up at her. A flick of its powerful tail sent it upward.

Tessa tried to scream. Her regulator fell out of her mouth and seawater rushed in. She choked and struggled to get the device repositioned.

The giant below her accelerated, growing in size. Its jaws started to open.

Something grabbed Tessa's right ankle, then her left. She was jerked out of the water and onto the dive boat.

Water sprayed over the divers and crew as the monster breached, maw gaping. The mouth snapped shut, hiding two sets of wicked teeth.

Tessa felt its cruel black eye on her as the beast crashed back into the water. She lay gasping and sobbing on the deck. Too weak to stand, Grace and Gibraltar helped her with her mask and tanks.

"What the hell was that?' Paul shouted, grabbing the railing as the boat bobbed violently in the monster's wake.

"Go! Go! Go!" the divemaster yelled at the captain.

Wasting no time, he pushed the throttle, and they retreated at top speed to the shore.

Tessa sat curled on the couch, a fleece throw wrapped around her shoulders.

Levi handed her a mug of tomato soup. "Please, babe. I need to know what you saw down there."

Tessa had barely spoken in the two weeks since the ordeal. Paul had taken her to the hospital to be checked out. The doctors said she was fine.

She was not fine. 202

"The report said a huge shark—"

"It was *not*... a shark."

"Then what was it?"

"You'll think I'm crazy."

He sat down and twisted sideways to face her. "You are not crazy." He petted her foot, which peeked out from under the blanket. "You might be surprised by what I would believe. Start with the shipwreck. Tell me about that."

Tessa tried her soup, but it was too hot. She set it on the coffee table.

Levi opened his arms, and she nestled against his chest. He stroked her hair.

"I'm not crazy."

"I know you aren't. What did you see?"

The words came tumbling out—discovering Tubi; the research grant; going back the second day and hearing the song; Robin's death; the thing she suspected was a mosasaur. Once the dam broke, she couldn't stop herself.

Tessa sniffled. "I think... I did something terrible."

"No. It wasn't you. It wasn't your fault."

Tessa choked back a sob. "But you've seen what's been happening. Whole fishing fleets lost. Whales sinking boats—and not just any whales. After that one survivor's description of an oversized light grey sperm whale with foot-long teeth, I'm sure it's *livyatan melvillei*. They lived during the Miocene. I mean, if there's a mosasaur in the Gulf of Mexico..."

"And how is any of this your fault?"

Tessa drew circles on Levi's chest with her index finger while she composed her thoughts. "So, the first day at the wreck, when I met Tubi, I wished that my research mattered. When we got back on the boat, Paul said that not only had the grant I wrote been awarded, but that a shipping company was matching the funding so they could figure out ways to stop whale-ship collisions."

"And that's bad how?"

"Paul emailed me yesterday. The company wants to test an aversion technology that blasts sound from the ships to chase the whales away. But it is at a volume and frequency that will damage their hearing, and maybe even kill them. And since they paid to be on the project, there is nothing I can do to stop it."

"You didn't do that."

"No? What about on the second day, when I wished that all the human-caused pollution would end, and the seas would thrive? All of a sudden, extinct creatures come out of nowhere and start wreaking havoc. It isn't safe to go anywhere near the water. I made two wishes that went horribly wrong."

"Listen to me!" Levi hissed. He lifted her chin, forcing her to look him in the eye. "None of this is your fault. Seventy-two B is not what you think it is. It's not some magic wishing whale that's all rainbows and puppies. It's a MALF—a Modified Alien Life Form. Created under Project Rastaban. It's. Dangerous. It could not be controlled."

Tessa jerked herself away from him. "How? How do you know about this?"

It was Levi's turn to go silent. He sighed heavily and buried his face in his hands. When he finally raised his head, his eyes had hardened, and his look was grim. "There's a chance we can fix this. I'm going to let you in on some history—Above Top Secret, Eyes Only history. If we survive this, you must tell no one. Not your mother, not your sister, not Grace, Paul, or Gibraltar. Do you understand?"

Tessa nodded.

Levi got to his feet and began to pace back and forth in front of the coffee table. "The Pentagon runs an unbelievable number of buried-many-levels-deep-secret projects. Stuff not even DAR-PA knows about, and that's saying something."

Tessa picked up the mug of soup, as if holding it between her and her agitated husband were some kind of defense against whatever horrifying story he was about to tell.

"The moon has no atmosphere, so meteors don't burn up before they hit it. A few of the rocks brought back from the various moon missions had what amounts to alien DNA tucked inside the crevices. It's different from ours, but generally works the same way."

"I think I can guess where this is going. Have none of these people seen *Jurassic Park*?"

"I agree. Through some complicated process I had no hope of understanding, they figured out what existing animals were most compatible with which type of ET DNA. 72B was most similar to an orca. So they CRISPR'd together his fragments with killer whale DNA and grew a monster."

Tessa pulled the afghan around her shoulders. "That just seems so... incredibly...."

"Stupid?"

"That, too."

"And there were presumably at least 71 others?" She took a sip from her cup.

"That information was on a need-to-know basis, and they didn't think I needed to know. Still, I had the impression that most of the other experiments didn't take."

"That's so messed up, Levi."

"Tell me about it. When my CO first recommended me and I got on the project, what they were doing seemed so amazing. But after I'd been on board a while and seen... the results." Levi frowned. "I wanted off."

Tessa had more soup.

"As I said, I don't know what any of the others were like, or even if they made it, but 72B was the worst thing I've ever seen. He gets inside your head."

She thought of the strange song Tubi had mesmerized her with. "You said his DNA was extraterrestrial. Do the scientists know where he came from?

"If they'd asked me, I'd have said Hell. But somehow, they figured it was from a planet near the Cat's Eye Nebula."

"Yeah. I mean he does have telepathy, and he showed me a vision of space, presumably close to his home world. But it isn't that bad, is it?"

Levi stopped pacing and looked at her. "Dr. Weingarten was the first one that we lost from the group. For whatever reason, 72B didn't like him. One afternoon, a two-man team from the security force saw the doctor walking down a passageway, muttering. That probably wouldn't have caught their attention, except for the meat cleaver he was carrying. They radioed the master-at-arms, and he told them to follow. Reinforcements were on route."

Tessa set her empty mug on the coffee table and stayed perched on the edge of the sofa.

"He bolted into the engine room and locked the door. Before the motorman could stop him, he whacked one of the high-pressure steam lines with the cleaver. He was cooked alive almost instantly. The motorman was badly burned but survived."

"And you think Tubi was responsible?"

Cliché or not, Tessa was both fascinated and terrified by the thought of seeing a monster shark that went extinct two million years before humans were a twinkle in Gaia's eye.

The shiny, dark grey tips of the dorsal fin and tail broke the water. And kept coming. Its wide back just breaking the surface, Tessa estimated the top fin was a little over five feet tall. The beast was nearly twice as long as the 40' fishing boat.

The fins disappeared.

"Oh, shit!" Levi grabbed the railing with one hand and Tessa's arm with the other. The Hippocamp lifted a few feet out of the water and both of them tumbled into the navigation equipment.

"Ow!" Blood oozed from a wrist-to-elbow scratch on Tessa's forearm.

Levi pushed the throttle. "It's trying to capsize us!"

"No, I don't think so. Just testing the boat to see if it's edible."

"We're edible, if it sinks us."

He wasn't wrong.

"Here it comes again!" Levi kicked the Hippocamp into reverse.

Tessa's eyes snapped to the six foot black dorsal fin slicing through the water. "No. That's not the shark." Five more tall fins rose above the glassy sea. "Orcas! A pod of them."

"You're right. Only the dorsal, no tail. Maybe they'll keep it occupied while we deal with 72B."

"Bet they'll do more than that. Sharks are their favorite lunch."

The killer whales dived beneath the waves.

For some minutes, all was still. Then the water began churning and red billowed up to stain the waves.

The megalodon breached, the fluke of one whale in its teeth. The flesh tore and the smaller animal dropped into the sea. The shark followed but stayed near the surface.

"We've got to get out of here." Levi changed the heading of the boat, and they began to pull away.

Tessa swallowed hard as they sped up. This was a much bigger shark than any of the orcas could have encountered before. It was way more than they could handle. *Please, please just go!*

The waters boiled again. This time, the great shark thrashed as multiple killer whales sank their teeth into each of its pectoral fins. Working together, they flipped the shark on its back. The monster fish stilled. Sharks go into a trance if they're held upside down. The orcas would keep it immobile at the surface to suffocate it before they made their final move.

"Look, Levi! They got him. There's probably a bigger liver in that thing than the whole pod can eat."

"Well. Hopefully that's a good sign."

There was nothing much remarkable on the sea floor as Levi moved the *Hippocamp* back and forth to find the wreck of the *Mary Fitzgerald*. Tessa was not upset by this. She wasn't sure she'd be able to force herself into the water for another encounter with Tubi at this point.

"There it is!" Levi pointed triumphantly to the fish-finder screen.

"Yeah. There it is." Tessa didn't feel the same enthusiasm.

The plan was hastily conceived, risky, and, if she was completely honest, unlikely to succeed. But when Levi had attempted to contact his former CO on Project Rastaban, he'd hit a brick wall. There would be no help from them, and who else would believe this crazy story about talking space whales?

Tessa would take refuge in the wreckage, so nothing came up behind her from the ocean, and she'd be carrying a bang stick. It could kill a small shark, but probably wouldn't do much more than annoy Tubi.

While she was distracting the monster, Levi would tag him with a bomb. She didn't know where he'd gotten it and she didn't ask. They'd have fifteen seconds to take cover before Tubi became sushi.

If everything played out exactly right.

Levi and Tessa pulled on their wetsuits. He kissed her. "See you on the flip side." Then he put in his regulator and slid his mask down.

She shivered as he stepped into the water.

Tessa stood on the edge for what felt like minutes, her brain telling her not to get in that water. Finally, she let go and took the plunge.

The sea was different. Instead of being a barren wasteland, four-foot ammonites swam past her. A sea scorpion trundled along the seabed. The yellow-striped figure of her husband was vanishing into the shipwreck. As much as she wanted to sit and observe this primordial life, she hurried after him.

She was nearly to the broken hull when something large and dark moved to block her way.

Tubi.

He grinned at her, his murderous teeth gleaming in the blue depths. *Have you not gotten tired of this by now?*

Tessa treaded water in front of the sinister clouded eye. It was all she could do not to hyperventilate from sheer terror. *Mashed potato, mashed potato.*

Motion from her left made her turn her head.

The mosasaur had swum up over the edge of the shelf and was slicing through the water toward Tessa—fifteen tons of instant death.

Her mind blanked. Time slowed as she watched the gigantic lizard's maw open, and she gazed at its double rows of recurved teeth, one in its jaw and one on the roof of its mouth.

Nowhere to hide.

No chance to get away.

She scrunched her eyes together and hunched her shoulders. *Undo the wishes! Undo the wishes!* Somehow, she knew this was not enough. *I wish Project Restaban and MALFs never existed!* She screamed inside her head as she waited for impact.

Seconds passed.

Nothing happened. Tessa opened her eyes.

"Coffee's ready." Robin Fellowes popped two slices of bread into the toaster.

"Thanks, babe." His wife set the SCUBA tank next to her pile of luggage. Dr. Tessa Whitlock kissed her husband's cheek before pouring herself a cup of joe.

"Hope our dive goes well. What do you think we'll find?" He sipped his coffee.

She frowned at her arm. *What on Earth? When did that happen?* An angry red scratch ran from the outside edge of her elbow to the inside edge of her wrist, and she had no idea where it had come from. That seemed to happen to her a lot lately—waking up with strange scrapes or bruises. Dreams that dissolved into sand if she tried to touch them.

But something was different today. She didn't know what, or how. But she had the feeling that the world that greeted her this morning was fundamentally different from the one she closed her eyes to last night.

And that was just fine.

List of Fairy Tales
That Inspired These Stories

Bluebeard's Castle/The Robber Bridegroom

The Bremen Town Musicians

Cinderella

The Fisherman and His Wife

Hansel and Gretel

Jack and the Beanstalk

Little Red Riding Hood

Puss in Boots

The Red Shoes

Sleeping Beauty

Snow White

The Stolen Farthings

The Three Little Pigs

If you enjoyed this book, please consider leaving a review at your favorite book site. Reviews help other readers find and enjoy new books!

To explore more content from Artemis Greenleaf, A.B. Richards, and Holly Dey, please visit BlackMareBooks.com

www.ingramcontent.com/pod-product-compliance
Lightning Source LLC
Chambersburg PA
CBHW011433170626
46808CB00010B/3141